# WRITTEN
## *in*
# STONE

ALSO BY ROSANNE PARRY

*Heart of a Shepherd*
*Second Fiddle*

# WRITTEN
## *in*
# STONE

ROSANNE PARRY

RANDOM HOUSE 🏠 NEW YORK

Text copyright © 2013 by Rosanne Parry
Jacket art copyright © 2013 by Richard Tuschman
Map art copyright © 2013 by Luiz Vilela

Visit us on the Web! randomhouse.com/kids

Educators and librarians, for a variety of teaching tools, visit us at
RHTeachersLibrarians.com

*Library of Congress Cataloging-in-Publication Data*
Parry, Rosanne.
Written in stone / Rosanne Parry. — 1st ed.
p. cm.
Summary: "A young girl in a Pacific Northwest Native American tribe in the 1920s must deal with the death of her father and the loss of her tribe's traditional ways."—Provided by publisher.
Includes bibliographical references.
ISBN 978-0-375-86971-6 (trade) — ISBN 978-0-375-96971-3 (lib. bdg.) —
ISBN 978-0-375-98534-8 (ebook) — ISBN 978-0-375-87135-1 (pbk.)
1. Makah Indians—Juvenile fiction. [1. Makah Indians—Fiction.
2. Indians of North America—Northwest, Pacific—Fiction. 3. Orphans—Fiction.
4. Northwest, Pacific—History—20th century—Fiction.] I. Title.
PZ7.P248Wr 2013 [Fic]—dc23 2012012491

Printed in the United States of America

10 9 8 7 6 5 4 3 2 1

First Edition

Random House Children's Books supports
the First Amendment and celebrates the right to read.

For my fifth-grade class at Taholah Elementary—
Ancy Grover, Ilene Terry, Phyllis Comenout,
Corinne Snell, Rosie Dan, Jeremy Mail,
Chris Baller, Jeffrey Capoeman, Anthony Seymour,
Shiva Capoeman, Greg Martinez,
Johnny Eselin, and David McCrory—
who asked for a book of their own. I never forgot, and
after all these years, this story is for you and all of your
children and even someday your grandchildren.

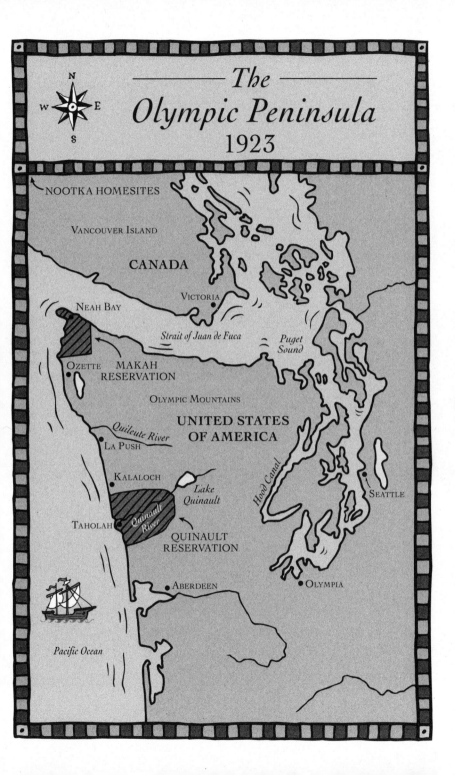

The Olympic Peninsula
1923

N W E S

NOOTKA HOMESITES

VANCOUVER ISLAND

CANADA

VICTORIA

NEAH BAY

Strait of Juan de Fuca

Puget Sound

OZETTE

MAKAH RESERVATION

OLYMPIC MOUNTAINS

UNITED STATES OF AMERICA

Quileute River

LA PUSH

KALALOCH

Lake Quinault

TAHOLAH

Quinault River

QUINAULT RESERVATION

Hood Canal

SEATTLE

ABERDEEN

OLYMPIA

Pacific Ocean

# MAY 1999

I don't need my eyes to tell me what's coming, and I don't need my great-granddaughter's hand on my elbow to keep me from stumbling. I know my way to the beach. For eighty-nine years, these feet have known the land of my tribe. I won't fall now. Not today. Not after waiting so long.

I let Ruby guide me, my grandson's girl, proud to have the honor of bringing old Pearl to the whale, our whale. She takes me at an easy pace, one hand under my arm and the other holding her drumsticks. She taps some hip-hop tune from the radio on the leg of her jeans. She doesn't hear the sound of death in that beat: the death cough of white disease, the gasp of a drowning man. She only knows it makes her father crazy when she taps it on the walls of their house.

On the beach, the shouting of reporters from Seattle,

Vancouver, and Victoria drowns out the sound I've been waiting for, praying for. But the wind brings something I have forgotten, the smell—sharp like smoke, but clean—of a whale. My hands tremble because I feel it rise up in me, one of the old songs, the one that welcomes the whale home. I lift my head and let it out. Ruby chants in, but the Makah words halt in her mouth as if she were a baby.

There was a time when we all knew this song. There was a time when we were kings of the ocean, and travelers told grand stories about our wealth of furs, copper, and whale oil. I remember the last time we sang this song. It was after the Great War, before the vote, before roads and radio and power lines took us places we did not imagine we would go. I was thirteen years old, as stubborn as any nose-pierced, black-leather-wearing, drum-playing great-granddaughter of mine.

I remember that girl.

# MARCH 1923

# 1

# *Waiting for the Whale*

I should have been praying that spring day. I should have been fasting for a successful whale hunt, but I was running. I ran along the wet sand with a harpoon in hand. The gray whale raised up his barnacle-speckled head, and raised it again to offer his life for the life of the tribe. I planted my feet and hurled the harpoon.

Thunk! My stick hit the log dead center and splashed into the sea.

I shouted in triumph and stamped my bare feet at the edge of the waves. A dozen steps into the whale dance, I froze. Dancing was forbidden during a whale hunt, and singing too. My father depended on it. I imagined him standing at the bow of the whaling canoe while my uncle and cousins paddled. He would hold his harpoon ready.

The round cedar bark hat would shade his weather-lined eyes: my papa, Victor Carver, the best whaler of the Makah, probably the best Indian whaler on the whole Pacific coast.

He would find us a whale, find one when no one else could. I pictured him leaping and striking and pulling the cedar rope. No depth or speed or strength would outlast him. He would bring home thousands of pounds of meat and hundreds of barrels of oil to feed our village and light our lamps. Sea captains knew his name and anchored off our shore to buy oil for cash money.

I looked over my shoulder. Behind me was my village; its arc of homes, boats, totem poles, and fish racks was pressed in the narrow place between waves and cedars. Only one house was traditional, with long cedar planks; the others had shingles and windows. But old or brand-new, every front door faced the ocean.

My grandfather's house was the best in the village. Our Whale crest in red and black paint covered the wall on the north side of the door, and our Raven crest covered the south. Totem poles marked the corners and doorways of our home. Everyone else lived in tiny matching houses with glass windows and the same color siding. But I was a princess. My father and grandfather were Makah whalers, and my mother was a Tlingit princess from the northern tribes, a weaver of the famous Chilkat blankets. We kept the traditions, the old stories, songs, and dances.

I saw my grandma coming down the beach toward me. Her limp made her roll when she walked, like a bear with a belly full of salmon. She was a Quinault from the south, married into the Makah as my mother had married in from the north. Sometimes I thought I was her favorite grandchild, but I was never sure. She had a bear's temper. I brushed sand off my hands and waited.

"Never turn your back on the ocean, Pearl. What if it decided to roll your whale up there with the other beach logs?"

She tilted her head in the direction of the great pile of twisted driftwood at the top of the beach. They were bleached white and worn smooth from sun and salt. I shrugged and turned away from her, wondering if she had seen me doing a man's dance.

"Walk with me," she said. "The tide's turned, and Charlie's waiting for you at the watching place." We turned our faces north, and I schooled my steps to match hers.

"Have there ever been women whalers?" I blurted out.

"Never," she said without pause. She put a calloused hand on my shoulder and leaned for a moment to rest her injured foot. "A woman's work is hard enough. Why are you borrowing burdens?"

"Women did plenty of men's work during the war, at the mills and the cannery and on the railroad. I could be a great whaler."

Grandma turned to me, her face a closed shell. "That war was poison to us, and nothing good came of it. We should divide work the way we always have."

I kicked at the sand. "Why don't I get to have adventures?"

"Shush! Shush your complaining, Pearl. We are waiting for a whale. We set aside our quarrels. We strive to be worthy."

"But it's not fair!"

"It's not lucky. Not respectful. We need this whale; you know we do. Now climb up that lookout. Charlie's been up there for hours." Grandma pressed a bundle of smoked salmon wrapped in a maple leaf into my hand. "And mind your *quelans*."

I trudged down the beach to the spit of sand and small rocky tide pools that connected the sea stack to the shore. At high tide, the rugged thumb of rock would be an island, but now I could walk across the sand without getting wet and climb the trail, as steep as a ladder, to the spot a hundred feet over the water where we watched the ocean.

My cousin Charlie looked up when I reached the top.

I could tell he was relieved to be done with his hours of sitting still, doing nothing but looking at the water. Charlie was born the same month as me, and we were equal back to back but he wanted to be taller than me. His father was the navigator. His brother, only seventeen, was already a whaler. Charlie was Grandpa's favorite, a drummer. Someday he would be a great singer.

But I was taller, because my father was the harpooner, the leader of the whalers, and Charlie knew it. He tried to tease me with mimes of the animals he'd seen while he was watching. He wanted me to scold him or laugh or do some other dishonorable thing at the watching place while the whalers were out. I gave his hair a yank and nudged him toward the beach. He walked away with a waddle in his step like Charlie Chaplin at the movies. Grandpa may have thought that Charlie would grow up to keep all his sacred songs, but I knew he really wanted to be a jazz singer, a movie star, a hunter of applause. No wonder the whalers didn't return while he was watching.

I breathed in the forest smells from the hills above the village. Broad cedars, blue-green spruce, and the nodding tops of hemlock trees stood shoulder to shoulder on the hillside. The fog lifted and it was a clear-enough day to see a dozen miles down the coast to the offshore rocks where my father and uncle hunted seals. A sea stack to the north marked the entrance to Shipwreck Cove and the burn-scarred hillside behind it, where I was forbidden to go. In the hills behind me were the trails I took every spring to the berry fields and camas meadows.

I turned my face west to the level blue-gray ocean and listened to the voices of gulls and the slow rhythm of waves rocking against sand and stone. I settled on the cedar mat and set my eyes to watching, but Grandma's words about *quelans* rang in my mind. Was I being disrespectful? I wished my cousin Henry was not out with the whalers. He always knew what to do about the things Grandma and Grandpa said, and I could count on him to be on my side. Still, they'd needed an eighth man. It was not so easy to get enough kinsmen together to run a whaling canoe, not since the war.

I thought over my conduct in the three days since Papa left. I had made my words honest and my body strong. I had settled my arguments. I had not complained . . . but I had been lonely. The room in the corner of Grandpa's longhouse that Papa and I shared was dreary with him gone. The empty space hung over my dreams. Older dreams, dreams I fought off years ago, came back in that empty room in the dark. Dreams of my mother.

Five years had passed since her death. Five years since the soldiers came home from the war in Europe with their tan uniforms, cooking-pot helmets, burn scars, and influenza. My mother and our baby were sick for two days. They sweat rivers of salt with the fever, and then fell to gasping like a drowning person on dry land. They could not speak or even cry. We were a hundred strong in this village to welcome our soldiers home. A month later, there were sixty-one graves.

I could not let myself think of that. I made myself think of waves and whales' voices and my father coming home. I drank rainwater from the cedar box. The sun was a few hours up from the horizon. I measured four hands between the setting sun and the calendar rock. *Panjans*, Grandma would call it, the last month of the year. March, they would call it at the schoolhouse up Neah Bay, Lent.

"I do not need to repent," I said aloud. The whales were hard to find, but I could not believe that God would punish us. Hadn't we given up our brutal traditions years ago? Slavery and raiding were not even a memory for me. We kept only the honorable customs. The Bible took its place with the most important stories. We had nothing to atone for. Still, the whalers had never been gone so long. I wondered if the sickness that followed our soldiers home from the war had settled in the ocean. Had the whales sickened and died? Had they disappeared as so many of our villages had? It took a year of prayer, sacrifice, and burning to clean the village after the influenza left. How could you clean the whole ocean?

The shadows grew longer, and I stood and swung my

arms to keep off the chill. Far out and to the north, I saw a black stick on the horizon. My heart beat faster. I waited and hoped and prayed.

When I could clearly see the tall curved prow and tail of my father's whaling canoe, I dashed for the trail down to the beach.

"The whalers are home!"

The joy of their return pulsed through my body. They were home, and I saw them first, and I would shout the news. It was so perfect that the stones on the path did not bruise my feet, and the nettles I brushed past did not raise welts. There was only the news and my voice shouting.

At the foot of the sea stack, I skidded to a halt. The tide had come up and covered the way to the beach, but I saw sand a foot under the water, so I drew a breath, and when the wave went out, I jumped. Salt splashed up and stung my eyes. I gathered my dress above my knees and ran for the shore. A wave crashed above my waist and drenched my clothes. I fought to find footing. The tug of the retreating wave made me stumble. I scrambled to my feet in the moment between one wave and the next and dashed up the beach. I took the porch steps in a single bound.

"Grandpa! They're home!" I called, rushing to his workbench. He looked up from the mask he was painting.

For a moment, a smile spread across his moon-round face, but then he put on his stoic leader-of-ceremonies look. He set his work aside and went to the massive chests at the back of the house to get out his regalia.

Aunt Loula didn't even try to be dignified. She scooped me and my cousin Ida into a hug and let tears fall. She and Ida hustled off to their treasure chests to make themselves fine. Ida was already begging after this robe and that cedar crown.

I ducked into my room and kicked off my wet clothes. I took my best town dress off the peg and brushed out my hair. There was no regalia for me in my father's carved and painted cedar chest. Years ago I had outgrown the button blanket my mother had made for me. I wore it far too long, dancing with it when it barely covered my knees. Last year, when it wouldn't reach below the tips of my fingers, I knew I had to set it aside. Papa had promised me a new button blanket after we sold the whale oil. He traced out the pattern on heavy brown paper and promised a hundred dozen pearl buttons. Even though I didn't have regalia of my own, I walked to the beach with my head high. I was the daughter of whalers.

The whole village assembled in rows, families of whalers first and all the others behind. Tall cedar hats showed who among us had hosted a giveaway. Red-and-black button blankets announced our lineage. The whale must know he gave himself for prosperous people. A rendering kettle was set to boil, and the drums and rattles were ready to sing. The long canoe pulled past the watching rock at the north end of the village and turned for the beach.

No whale.

The drums faltered and fell silent. The welcome song waited in my mouth. Seven silhouettes bent over their paddles. There was no shout or raised arms, no trail of seabirds and sharks. Grandma counted, *"Pau, saali, chakla, muus..."* She wept before she came to seven. I did not count. I knew where the harpooner sat. My body held still as stone, but my mind flew out over the ocean like a seagull looking north and south, crying in a gull's one-note voice.

Gone. Gone. Gone.

## 2

# *The Forbidden Feast*

A condolence call was what the Indian agent called it when he came two days later with his fast boat and fat mustache. He ran his boat up on the sand without a proper greeting or invitation. He looked around the beach for a few minutes, licking his thin lips, hoping to find something he could confiscate and then sell to the curio shop in town. He said he was here to pay his respects. He even remembered to remove his hat. I was suspicious already.

"I am sorry for the loss of Mr. Carver, a good man."

The Mustache went on for many sentences, dishonoring us with the free use of a dead man's name. Grandpa and Uncle Jeremiah met him on the beach, and I stood behind Grandpa's shoulder, ready to translate words from English to Makah or read legal papers out loud.

They spoke to the agent as honorably as they would any visiting chief, but Charlie went up to the watching rock to see if he had brought policemen, and Henry took men into the house to load rifles.

The agent went on in a fair-weather voice. Did we need the missionary? Should he send for a Black Robe? Could he take the orphan to school for us?

"It's a fine Indian school with a long tradition, Chemawa in Oregon," he said. "The girl would learn a trade. She would make a comfortable life, a domestic in some fine house in Portland or Seattle. It's a bright future for this poor, fatherless girl, and a burden off your shoulders."

Grandpa looked at me, and I did not know how to translate. There was no word for *orphan* in Makah. I paused to think of how to say this thing. I bit at the inside of my cheek to hurry the right word along.

"He thinks I am a helpless child with no home to live in and no future," I said to Grandpa. And then I whispered, "But he doesn't mean it." Because I could see that Grandpa must challenge a man who said he is not able to care for his own grandchild, as if he were a slave and not a chief.

Uncle Jeremiah pretended to laugh. "Take our Pearl away from her grandmother? It would break the old woman's heart."

And then I laughed because there was nothing on my grandma that was going to break. She was solid through.

The Mustache nodded and pretended to look sad. "I loved my granny too," he said, and he looked me over as you might a fish at the market. "She can go to the school next year. It's not too late for her to progress. She has English, at any rate, and that's the most important thing."

"As you wish," Uncle Jeremiah said, because there was nothing an agent loved so much as a humble Indian.

"But a preacher," the Mustache went on. "You must have one for a proper burial. Who shall I send?"

When I translated, I said the word *burial* with extra strength because we all knew there was no body, and why would he care how we bury a body we didn't have, and why had he come to offer condolence when he was not sad to see an Indian die.

Grandpa looked up the beach to where Charlie was waving "all clear" from the watching rock, and Henry stood ready in front of the longhouse. Today, luck was on our side, and the agent was only there to warn us. He knew we were going to chop a hole in the bottom of Papa's whaling canoe. He knew we would lay his harpoon and whaling gear inside and raise it on posts with the prow facing west. He knew there would be a feast and guests and a giveaway. My grandfather would die of shame to not give his son an honorable memorial. But the law forbade the potlatch.

Last year, the chiefs of the Kwakiutl went to jail. They spent months locked in the pigsty at the federal prison, and all their regalia—the masks, robes of power, head-dresses, and eagle down—were confiscated and carried off to a museum in Canada.

The Mustache knew we would try to potlatch. He tugged at his face hair the way an otter does. I could see him calculating the odds on how many officers he would need to arrest us all, and how he would find the giveaway or know the day we held it. Uncle Jeremiah stood shoulder to shoulder with Grandpa and stared the man down. They had tried to kill the potlatch here and in Canada for a generation. The potlatch had not died.

"See that you put him away properly," the Mustache said.

Grandpa answered, "It will be properly done."

They shook hands on the agreement, and then he left with his fast boat and bad smell.

Grandpa spit out that promise as soon as he was gone, and Uncle Jeremiah said, "Don't worry, Pearl. Your father was a great man. We will honor him with a feast, and a hundred years from now people will remember his deeds. No one will go home with an empty hand."

\* \* \*

The next weeks were a rush of gathering. There would be hundreds of people to feed, blankets to buy, masks and drums and songs to make ready. But this time there were no goods stacked up to the roof of the house, no moving furniture to make room for piles of gifts. Instead, I watched the men slip away after dark with loaded boats and lanterns. They were gone for hours but not overnight. Instead of sending a feast messenger by canoe, they sent a postal letter, a thing that could not be questioned or searched. They bought goods from a merchant who would not talk. I didn't need someone to spell it out for me. They were going to hold my father's potlatch in secret on an island, probably in a cave on Tatoosh. The Indian agent would not think to look there. But when I offered to help, to hold the lantern or prepare the dance floor, Uncle Jeremiah brushed me aside. Only the men would go. Only the men would risk jail.

If I had been younger, I would have pouted, run to Grandma and complained. But this time, for once, I kept my own council and made my own plan. I just wanted something of my father's to keep, something small from his regalia that I could always have close to me. Something like the abalone shell from my mother's button blanket.

I put a hand to the pouch I kept at my waist under my dress. If Mama had died in childbirth, or of an accident as Papa had, they would have packed up her regalia, her button blanket and headdress, her jewelry and ceremonial things. They would have kept them in a cedar chest for me and for my daughters. But my mother died in a time of fear. The newspapers said the influenza was our fault for living too many people in one house.

"Unsanitary," the newspaper said.

"Unnatural," the missionary said, and he left us and never came back.

"You must burn the bodies," the Indian agent said. "Or the disease will never leave your village."

My father did the burning. He carried the bodies to the fire, with the baby in Mama's arms. I could not watch. I hid in the drift logs on the beach, too sick at heart even to weep. When their bodies were gone, he built up the fire again and called me to bring their things, every toy and tool and piece of clothing. His face was smudged with soot and his eyes were strange, like the wild man mask I had seen at a potlatch the summer before.

"We can't hold on to them," he told me. "If we keep their things, even one little thing, a needle, a handkerchief, they will never be free, and we will never be free of them. Their death will call to us until we lose our minds and go to death with them."

I had seen it happen. A woman burned the body of her fifth child, and then she gathered up all her children's clothing, their shirts and small dresses, and hugged them to her body. She walked into the deep forest and did not walk out.

Papa's hands shook as he put each of Mama's things in the fire, the cradle and the clothes, the sewing pouch and the spindle. I tried to hold my mother's button blanket back. I wanted it to be mine. I wanted to wrap myself in her clan symbols and feel their protection in the dark. But Papa found the chest with her ceremonial things and dragged the entire box to the fire. I couldn't let him do it, but I couldn't stop him either. At the last minute, when no one was looking, I grabbed Papa's fish knife and cut one of the abalones from the border of Mama's button blanket, a glass-smooth, palm-sized piece of shimmering purple shell.

For years, I tucked it under my cheek to help me sleep and defend me from bad dreams, and it did speak to me and call up memories of my mother. I loved that voice. And I wanted something of Papa's, a feather from his Raven mask or a piece of the cedar fringe, to speak to me in his voice.

At the giveaway, Grandpa would take Papa's masks and dance robes and all the songs and dances and stories that were his to tell, and he would give them away or keep them for my sons and grandsons. It was better than burning, but they are not a woman's dances, and his regalia would never come to me. All I needed was a chance to see his masks and dance robes one last time and find some small part of it to keep.

It took almost a week to get my plan together. There was a fish canoe, a little one I could paddle by myself. I put together a disguise, not a perfect one, but I would be paddling in the dark. I went over the landmarks on the way to the island, the ones I would be able to see in the moonlight. I practiced my paddling whenever I had a spare moment. It was risky, but I had to try.

The morning before the feast, I spent the whole day with raw fish. The fog had rolled in and cut the houses from my sight. Henry was painting the new totem pole with Uncle Jeremiah. Charlie was making a drum with Grandpa and rehearsing the welcome song. Even little Ida was making baskets for the giveaway. It was just talentless me, and the dead fish.

I could hear the littlest cousins running gutted fish to the alder fire where the Quinault aunties roasted it on sticks over a long pit in the sand, red meat facing red coals. I wore Grandma's apron and used her knife. My cut fingers burned where salt water touched them. I hated gutting fish. My mother never made me do it, not alone. I picked up a Blueback salmon as long as my arm and spoke to his silver blank eyes.

"I bet you have places you'd rather be."

Whack.

"If I could weave like my mother—"

Slice.

"Or make a basket like every single one of my aunties—"

Scrape. Scrape.

"In fact, if I had any talent at all—"

"If you had any *quelans* at all, you'd treat our salmon with more respect!" Grandma stepped into my circle with a look fiercer than I had ever seen.

I jumped and dropped the knife in the gut pile. I knew what she was going to say. It fell on me like winter rain.

"They will not come back," she said. "If you treat our salmon with disrespect, they won't come back to our river. Every year, they have offered their lives for us, for a hundred generations."

I sifted through the gut pile and lifted the goopy knife. I flicked a stray scrap of skin off the meat. Grandma winced, but she saw I was trying.

"It's not healthy to work alone," Grandma said. She took a knife from her apron pocket and lifted the cedar mat that kept the seagulls from stealing the catch. She cradled the salmon in one hand and whispered a Quinault blessing.

She made one long slice down the spine, two scrapes and a chop. Perfect. I would never get it right.

Grandma looked at me and laughed. She leaned over and gave me a little shove with her shoulder.

"Yah, yah, if you clean fish this good, we start looking for a husband."

I picked up another fish and sliced it open even more crookedly, then turned away so she wouldn't see me smile. There was plenty of time to get good at cleaning fish later.

# 3

# *The Giveaway*

The next day was cold and clear. I stood at the door to greet the guests. Uncle Royal and his sons were out in the powerboats looking for the Indian agent. Uncle Royal was the perfect spy. He cultivated a reputation with the white fishermen. He was the Cheerful Indian. He shook hands firmly and laughed at their jokes loudly and gossiped with them about other Indians. All last week, he had bragged about the big "do" among the Quileute to the south of us. But when the Mustache went there, he would only find old McCreedy and his traveling flea market.

McCreedy was the longest-talking Indian in the world. He could talk the legs off a snake, which is why you never see one walking around. He would corner the

Mustache and give him information in lavish detail about the real potlatch up across the sound with the Nootka on Vancouver Island. When the Mustache headed up north, feeling clever about the inside information he'd managed to wheedle out of that old man, McCreedy would run to the long-bearded customs agent. His boat was faster. If all went according to plan, the Beard would catch the Mustache, and they would fight, maybe even fist-fight, over taxes and jurisdiction and international border, and they would be fifty miles away from our potlatch. Uncle Royal laughed, already imagining it. He was the last guest. He hugged me off the ground as my father used to do, then closed the longhouse door.

The house was completely different set for a feast. The partitions that separated sleeping rooms from the rest of the house, and the worktables where Grandpa carved and Grandma and Aunt Loula twined their baskets, were moved out of the way. Long feast tables and benches were set for a hundred and fifty guests in two rows down the middle of the house, with extra tables around the edge. The Whale and Wolf feast dishes ran the length of the tables. Each one was as big as the bathtub in the Sears catalog. Smaller dishes were passed for guests to take their fill. We served salmon and halibut, oysters, potatoes, littleneck clams, salmonberry cake, elk steak, fry bread, blue mussels, bear sausage, canned peaches, biscuits, huckleberry jam, urchins, peas, and candy.

Grandma and Aunt Loula walked among the guests, passing out strings of olive shell, small enough to hide in a pocket. They explained to each man where to find the secret giveaway. I squeezed in next to my friends, Anita and Dorothy from Nitinat and Alert Bay. Charlie was across the table with his pack of cousins, and Henry leaned his head toward a young lady from the Queen Charlotte Islands.

Anita handed me a plate stacked tall with all my favorite foods and a full ladle of eulachon grease poured over the top. But the smell of the food and the press of so many people close together was too much for me. The last time we feasted in Grandpa's house, my mother was alive. She sat across the table from me, and I held the baby in my lap picking out berries, biscuits, and soft potato for her tender mouth.

I tried to put them out of my mind and listen to the talk around me, but I could not swallow. I chewed and chewed, but the food would not go down. I would dishonor my father to sit at his feast table and not eat. Grandpa sat at the head of the table. He noticed everything. I prayed he would notice who was flirting with Henry or the swear Charlie learned from a logger, and not me. My mouthful of food felt bigger and bigger, and my hands started to sweat.

Aunt Loula slid in beside me on the bench. She patted my back as if I were a baby. She chatted at me about her family.

"Look at all those girls flirting with my Henry. Maybe he'll make a match today. Charlie will sing later. He's so talented. And look how tall my Ida's grown. She was only a baby the last time we had a feast here."

I hated her and her living family. She had never lost anything in her life. She couldn't possibly understand me.

"Blue mussel?" she said to Anita. "Your favorite, right?" She scooped a bit of my food to Anita's plate.

"This is the finest sausage we've made in years," she said, helping herself to mine. She went on in praise of her own cooking and passed around my food until salmon was uncovered. She leaned in and whispered, "Salmon is familiar. It goes down." She gave me a final pat and flapped off to crow at someone else.

Ida slid in beside me next. She bounced on the bench, making my already queasy stomach worse.

"Sisters," she hissed through missing front teeth. "We'll be real sisters now. Mom said you can move into my room. Girls aren't supposed to live alone. Besides, Henry's old enough to take a bride. Dad and Grandpa said he can live in your room, and you can share mine.

You can have the top bunk if you want, and I'll let you use my crayons."

I didn't hate Ida yet, but I could see it coming.

After the feast came the story. Uncle Jeremiah told it standing tall in his black-and-red robe of power in front of the carved panels of Whale and Raven. He sprinkled oil on the fire to make it burn brighter. The guests settled in silence.

"Our whale hunt began beautifully," he said. "We saw spouts to the northwest, but as we drew near, the whales dove and disappeared. Before, when we met our brothers on the open sea, they raised up their heads to greet us. In time, one would swim alongside our canoe and offer his life for us. But this time, the whales ran from us without even a raised head in greeting.

"Had we offended them? Had we come to hunt with greed in our hearts? Disrespect in our minds? We prayed and searched, traveling farther from home.

"The morning of the second day, we found a whale alone, a singer, a humpback. He had many notches along his tail from battles with killer whales. This old one greeted us in the traditional way. His body rose beside the canoe, and we saw scars. Deep gashes ran from the blowhole down to the tail. Some scars were old, but one was so fresh it bled. They were as deep and jagged as the scars a bear leaves on the bark of a tree.

"My brother stood with his harpoon ready. As he lunged to strike, my son, Henry, shouted for him to stop, a direct challenge, a break in our silence."

There was a stir among the listeners. The old whalers from Neah Bay and Vancouver Island leaned their heads together and spoke with sharp urgency. They had the power to cast Henry out from the society of whalers.

But the younger men and those from families that did not rank high enough to hunt whales looked at my cousin with admiration. I saw whispers pass among them and nods of satisfaction. If Uncle Jeremiah noticed the divided response, he gave no sign. He went on with the story.

"The old whale lifted his head one last time and dove. My brother saw the dive coming. He leapt from the boat to the whale, ready to drive the harpoon deep and end our whale's suffering. I did not see him strike.

"The whale pushed our canoe over with his tail and disappeared. We struggled to right our boat, to collect our paddles. Henry dove for his uncle in the dark water. My brother and the whale vanished, with no sound, bubble, or spout.

"We were alone on an empty sea. As we turned our canoe for home, my brother's harpoon floated up from the depths, snapped in two pieces.

"We paddled with heavy hearts, not guessing the sorrows ahead. That evening, we saw a ship. In the distance, we thought it was a steam-powered trader. Nearer, we took it for an ironclad navy vessel with a bow-mounted cannon.

"Then the truth became clear. It was a battleship making war on the whales. The cannon held a harpoon. Dead whales were pumped full of air, chained up, and dragged along behind, only to be eaten away by sharks. Twenty whales were pouring out their blood, and still they steamed after more. The waste! The dishonor! We wanted to curse their white greed, but these sailors had faces like ours. They flew the red sun of Japan. Hours later, we passed more battleship whalers, one from America, one from Russia. We saw more dead whales in one day than this village has seen in three generations."

Uncle Jeremiah stepped back, his tale finished. Anger rose in the room like the tide.

"Thieves!" a man shouted from one side. "The whales are ours to take."

Grandpa's deep voice rolled out every curse in every language he knew. "Liars! Treaty breakers! We gave them land for the sea!" he shouted. Grandpa holds the long pages of our treaty in his memory. "We gave them the trees, three hundred thousand acres of trees, theirs forever. All we asked for was the whales, and the right to hunt and fish as we always have. Now they scorn our treaty and steal the life out of the sea."

Under the high tide of anger I heard women's voices, quieter and more urgent, talking about hunger, disease, poverty, and shame.

Henry stood to speak.

"I broke our tradition of silence on the hunt. Maybe I was wrong to do it. Maybe my uncle's death is my fault. But I believe the old whale came to warn us, to show by his scars that the whales are leaving. Soon they will be gone forever, hunted out like the sea otters. What child younger than ten has seen a sea otter? They are all dead, and my children will never know their whiskered faces hiding in the kelp beds."

Henry's words broke over me like waves. I felt like a sinking stone. I wanted to feel heavy. I wanted to walk along the ocean floor. I wanted to look for my father in the houses of whales and seals. My father—the last whaler.

Grandma got up to speak. She went to the front by the fire. People stopped talking. They shushed the children. Grandma was a famous storyteller.

"I believe," she called out, as steady and strong as a revival tent preacher. "I believe the whales have seen the greed of the big whaling ships. They have gone deep, and they have taken my son, our finest whaler, with them. They will wait in the deep for men to change their ways. And we will wait with them.

"You, fathers, teach your sons the meditations of a whaler and the arts of ocean navigation. Mothers, teach your daughters the prayers of a whaler's wife and the ways to prepare whale meat."

People sat up taller as Grandma spoke. They lifted their heads, and I felt the power of her voice like that invisible force that made a flock of birds or a school of fish turn together as if they were one animal. I wondered for a moment, if there was no voice like hers, would we be a tribe at all?

"We will honor our whales," Grandma went on. "Even when they are gone from us we will honor them with our songs and dances, our carving and our stories. For I believe, I do believe our whales will come back to us one day."

After the feast, the men left, using the full moon to navigate. They slipped out in groups of four or six. They moved over the ocean as quiet as shadows in the light of the moon. I had to wait with the women for the fire to burn low and the chatting aunties to put their children to bed.

When everyone was busy, I sneaked outside and tip-toed down the porch, skipping the loud step. I went to the side of the house and pulled the fish canoe down the sand, the small one that I could paddle alone. I took an old spruce root hat and a wool blanket out of the canoe, where I had hidden them. With them on in the dark, I would look like one of the grandmothers. No one told the grandmothers what to do.

"Where will you go in the dark?" Grandma's sharp voice came from the shadows at the far end of the front porch.

I gasped, dropped the canoe on my foot, and cursed silently.

"Out," I said back just as sharp, and tugged the boat farther. I didn't have to look for her frown. I felt it. I didn't care; she couldn't stop me. I was stronger than she was. Anyone strong enough to stop me was already at the giveaway.

"Will I tell the Pitch Woman story again?" she said.

The name hit me like a slap, and the most horrifying details of the Pitch Woman story flooded my memory. I couldn't make myself look over my shoulder at the dark spaces between the trees. I leapt all five of the porch steps in one bound and stood in the stripe of lamplight that leaked out the door. Once I was in light, I could take a breath and close my mind to that story. I turned and studied the black water between me and my father's potlatch. My hands shook. I gave Grandma the same hard look she gave me. I had an urge to dash inside and bar the door. Leave her alone in the dark to face the Pitch Woman.

"It is not wrong to be angry," Grandma said.

I turned all the way around and faced her full on.

"It is not wrong that you want to be there," Grandma went on. "I want to be there too—he is my son." She gave me a quick peek at her own sorrow and then covered the wound carefully. I kept my sorrows bound up tight, but they bled anyway.

"If you are determined, Pearl, I will go with you," Grandma said. "I will carry the light, and you will paddle, and we will find the giveaway together or a jail in Vancouver together. But there is another way to go, a safer way."

I shrugged. Safer did not hold much appeal. Grandma waited me out.

I remembered how long it would take to paddle alone. "Safer?" I asked.

Grandma ducked inside and brought out a lamp. It cast a warm pool of light on the porch. We settled, backs against the wall.

"Who came to the feast today?" she asked.

I closed my eyes. "Shall I tell them by tribe or by order around the table?"

Grandma smiled, proud of my memory. "We'll start from Alaska and go south," she said.

I worked my way down the names and clan connections, and Grandma told me the gifts they would receive tonight, who made them, and why they went to that family.

I had only thought to keep something of my father's for my own comfort, not about this naming of gifts. Maybe twenty years from now, I would travel to a village I'd never visited before, but someone there would remember that I was the daughter of the whaler Victor Carver.

"I remember him," they would say, and they would think of the honor their family received tonight and treat me with respect. It was not the same as a thing I could hold, but it had a weight of its own.

Still, I wanted something, one small thing of my father's to keep for my own.

# 4

## *Summer at Lake Quinault*

The season for berries came, and the carved cedar boxes that held the whale meat and oil stood empty. We turned our backs to the ocean and traveled to the summer hunting places to meet Grandma's people, the Quinaults. They did not hunt whales. Their wealth and power and fame were in the Quinault River and the Blueback salmon, the richest meat fish of them all. To hear them talk about their salmon, you'd think they were whales.

Last year, we came to the lake after our whale hunt, fresh from selling the oil in town. We wore new clothes and carried new rifles and toys. We gave presents to all our relatives. This year, we came in lighter canoes. My dress showed a dark stripe at the hem and sides where Aunt Loula had let out the seams.

Aunt Loula took the occasion of our long trip, down the coast to Taholah and then up the river to Lake Quinault, to plan my future. When I was the only daughter of a great whaler, no one minded that I couldn't draw or weave or twine a basket, that I sang more like a bear than a bird. But I would have to learn something of value now that the power had gone out of my name.

Aunt Loula wanted me to learn baskets. Aunt Loula knew baskets. She had a reputation for turning out the small, close-woven ones with a colored pattern that sold at the curio shops in Seattle, Juneau, and San Francisco.

"You can get money for a good basket," Aunt Loula said. "Especially when you work out a deal with a regular buyer."

"Never very much money," I said. "You would have to turn out dozens a month to make it worth the trip to town."

"If you were good at it, you would be able to turn out a dozen baskets a month."

"Yes," I snapped. "And you know what an outstanding basket maker I am. Completely without form or balance, that's what you said about the last basket I made."

Aunt Loula opened her mouth to snap back at me, but then she sighed and arranged a calmer expression. "I didn't mean it."

"People say what they mean." I was not going to let up on her.

"You could learn," she said quietly. "You're plenty smart enough, but you don't pay attention to your work, Pearl. Your mind is miles away when you are making a basket. What are you thinking about all the time?"

I could feel her leaning forward and to one side in the canoe to look at my face. There was no way I was going to tell her what I was thinking. She wasn't my mother. I let an unpleasant silence grow between us. I heard Henry paddling more loudly behind his mother and felt a touch of guilt. He always took my side when Ida cheated at dice or Charlie copied my schoolwork. Even if I would never love Aunt Loula, I ought to respect her for his sake.

I was about to apologize when Aunt Loula said, "A woman with baskets can stay home with her family, not go off to some cannery job miles away."

I knew it was true, but I fought it. I wanted to be a weaver, as my mother had been. She had a commission from a chief up north. He was going to pay her a hundred trade blankets and seventy-five dollars in gold coin. It would take her a year to follow the pattern on the board this chief sent, but when she was finished, her Chilkat blanket would hold a place of honor in that chief's house for generations. That was what I wanted, something that would last. And Aunt Loula was right. I was a pathetic basket maker. Mine always came out flat as a plate and wobbly around the edges.

"Keep working," Grandma had said when I was younger. "It takes practice."

But I think she was relieved when I gave it up and learned to spin from my mother instead. It was the first step to becoming a weaver. It took forever to get the feel of stretching the wool out and rolling it up my thigh into an even twist of yarn. But Mama never minded my mistakes and never rushed me to be perfect. She laughed at my lumpy tangles and said, "Put some more meat on that leg and the spinning will go easier. Get outside and run. I won't have that Charlie running faster than my girl."

And then I would forget the weaving altogether and attack Charlie with a broken fish club. Pirates and Indians was our favorite game. If I had known that I'd lose Mama that same year, I would never have played outside, not ever. I would have sat beside her and watched her hands. Weaving was a rare gift—a legacy. It should have been mine, and I wanted it.

I fumed over Aunt Loula's words all the way up the river. I didn't rest. Not when the blisters rose, as we reached the mouth of the lake and paddled along the southern shore past the gravel bar at Willaby Creek. Not when they broke and oozed, as we paddled by the green sloping lawn and powder-blue rowboats at the Lake Quinault Lodge. There was something satisfying in the sharpness of the pain.

I watched the tourists lounging in chairs and playing croquet at the lodge. They never seemed to worry. They spent the whole day not working, unless you count rowing a lady with a parasol around in circles work. And then they went in that fancy dining hall for dinner without a care for how they would pay.

"What do you suppose they do, to eat without working?" I asked.

"Rob banks," Henry said. "Or maybe hold up trains. I am especially suspicious of those two." He pointed to a magnificently overweight gray-haired woman and her companion with a cane and thick spectacles.

Even Aunt Loula laughed.

"Look," I said, pointing to three boys in sailor suits digging in the sand. "Prospectors. No doubt they've struck oil or made their fortunes in gold already."

As we passed by, the boys stood up and pointed at our canoes. They pantomimed shooting us with arrows and made war whoops. In the canoe in front of us, Charlie pretended to shoot back, and Ida waved as if she were the belle of the Independence Day parade.

Last year, when we came to the camp on the meadow at the east end of the lake, Grandma's nephews teased

Papa and Uncle Jeremiah about the foolishness of chasing after whales in the ocean.

"If you wait long enough, one will wash up on your beach," they said. "No mess, no danger, just a free gift."

But when Papa told the story of how it was to touch a living whale out on the open sea, nobody laughed, and he held a place of honor at the summer feasting.

This summer was quiet. When our canoes pulled in, the Quinault relatives glanced up from their work and said *"Oo-nu-gwee-tu"* and nothing more. Everyone knew we had lost our whale. Everyone knew we were not alone in our troubles. None of the whaling families of Vancouver Island had seen a single whale on any of the usual ocean paths. There had been no feast messenger and no gathering of families to sing the praises of the whalers and share in the meat and oil. I missed visiting with my friends from Nitinat and Alert Bay, and I wondered if they felt the same spooky feeling of looking over the ocean and not seeing the spouts of whales.

Were the whales punishing us for not keeping the old ways? Would we suffer because other nations chose to hunt with disrespect? If it was true, there was no way for an Indian to live at all—put in prison by white men for keeping the old ways, and abandoned by whales for losing them.

I stepped onto the grass at the meadow, my arms

shaking from the paddling and my legs stiff from hours in the canoe. Aunt Loula took one look at my blistered hands and growled.

"Foolish girl," she hissed at me. "You ruin your hands when we have all this work to be done."

"I'll work," I said, holding my voice steady so I sounded more grown up than her. "I'll go up to the mountains and gather goat wool for my weaving."

I could see she was dying to tell me weaving was not real work, not useful work. "Fine," she said. "If Susi will take you."

I walked off with my head low so she would think she had won, but inside I was dancing. Aunt Susi, my favorite person!


That night, there was dancing under the summer constellations. The meadow grasses were tamped flat in a circle around the fire. The drummers and singers gathered. Robes of power were unpacked from cedar chests and suitcases. Uncle Jeremiah took his rifle for signaling and went out in the dark to watch the road. Ida and her little friends taught the grandmothers to sing the happy birthday song and giggled at their mistakes. It was Grandpa's turn to pretend to have a birthday. Charlie put a tall candle in a loaf of store bread.

"Listen, Grandpa," he said. "After everyone sings, you close your eyes and make a wish."

Grandpa listened carefully. "And do I sing? Tell a story?"

"No, all you have to do is blow out the candle."

"No dance? No magic? These people do not know how to make a proper feast."

"I've noticed," Charlie said. "They seem to prefer their celebrations very plain. But if we pretend it's a birthday party, we can even give gifts. The sheriff in these parts leaves Indians alone, so long as we are having a white person's party."

Other summers Aunt Loula brought carved and painted canoe paddles for me and Ida. We always did the paddle dance together to represent the Makah side of the family. But not this year. We would wait a whole year after my father died before we danced again.

But my Quinault kin brought out their best regalia and lined up to dance. Papa had promised me a new robe of power this year. He would have bought me wool and pearl buttons on our trip to town before we came to the lake. I would have worked on it all summer, with my aunts and girl cousins pitching in. It would have been a thing to gossip over and admire. When many women worked on a robe, each one put some of her strength in it. That strength would have been mine to wrap myself in, and mine to show at winter ceremonies. I had last year's coat from the store. It kept my skin dry, but it left my heart cold.

Aunt Susi came up behind me and gave my arm a squeeze. "I want you to wear this tonight for me," she said.

She unfolded her own button blanket. It was thick and heavy and reached to my feet. When Susi draped it over my shoulders, the firelight made the pearl buttons sparkle. It felt like putting on the stars.

The songs began and the younger girls had the first dance. My littlest Quinault cousin, Esther, was going to dance for the first time. Every eye was on her, but she was looking at me. As usual, I counted down the last six beats, signaling with my hand so Esther would start on the right beat. She was a good little dancer as soon as she forgot the watching eyes and remembered her feet. She swirled into the circle of firelight, and all her sisters and cousins followed her around the fire, each one three beats behind the dancer in front of her. I had known this dance by heart since I was five years old.

If my baby sister had lived, she would have danced it too. We would have practiced it over and over until every turn of the paddle and every swoosh of our robes matched perfectly. I remembered my father dancing the Raven stories in his carved cedar mask and feather-covered cape.

He would soar and dive and bank. People sat perfectly still to watch him, almost believing he could fly. No one else danced the entire cycle of Raven stories, from Raven Releases the Sun to Raven Scatters the Salmon Eggs. I imagined my sons learning those dances. Henry would have to teach them, or Charlie. They were not a woman's dances, but they would come to me to be sure every step was perfect. I was the one who would remember.

# 5

## *Gathering Wool*

Next morning, Aunt Susi led the way to the mountain meadows where trees grew waist-tall and mountain goats grazed. We walked together up an old hunting trail with two empty baskets and a long cotton sack. Susi was the oldest unmarried person I knew. The grandmothers shook their heads and clucked about how old she was. Twenty-five, at least, they said, as if she would turn gray any moment. But the young men watched her every step and swore she was in the bloom of nineteen years.

I knew for a fact Susi would be twenty-three on the fifth of the next month. I knew every birth and marriage in the family. I could recite all of Grandma's stories. I knew every dance and song my family owned, even the ones girls were not allowed to do. People counted on my memory.

Susi was the only auntie who could outrun me. I had to step lively to keep up with her, but she rested every time we crossed water so we could drink and I could bathe my blistered hands. She sat cross-legged on a rock in the kind of denim dungarees loggers wore. I just looked at her and laughed, a woman in pants. The uproar at the camp when she drove in that morning was worth a nickel to see.

"What's gotten into that Susi!" the aunts whispered to each other.

"Is that girl looking for a wife or a husband?" Uncle Royal boomed out.

Susi laughed. If she had a husband, they'd tease him for keeping an uppity woman. If she lived with family like a normal girl, her parents would get an earful on the subject of proper decorum. But Susi lived alone in the one-room apartment over the post office. She did all her own earning. It made the grown-ups crazy. I pictured myself wearing work pants to the schoolhouse up in Neah Bay. My teacher's skinny head would pop right off his body from the shock of it.

"Do you ever get lonely?" I asked. "Working at the post office by yourself?"

I'd wanted to ask this for a long time. Susi's man died in France in the war.

"Sometimes," Susi said. "If I think about it. If I try to hold on to what's not there."

There wasn't much in Kalaloch, the beach town where Susi lived, a few cottages for fishermen and their families, a bunkhouse for loggers, a sugar and flour store, and one farmer trying to keep pigs and chickens alive. I'd go crazy in such a little town with no one to talk to.

We got up and moved on, singing now because we were in bear territory. They would let us pass unharmed if we sang. I sang my father's whale chant and the ballad my mother sang to herself at the loom. Susi did ragtime tunes from the radio.

It was already past noon when we reached the alpine meadow. Pale green grass poked out of the rocky soil. Tall foxgloves shaded the gentians that hugged the ground. Gigantic boulders dotted the grass as if a giant had thrown them out like beaver-tooth dice. My hands tingled from the altitude, and I leaned over, resting hands on knees to catch my breath. The meadow was empty of animals, but it took only a few minutes to find a mound of wet black beads—goat scat.

"Fresh," Susi said, pointing to flies that buzzed and hovered. We followed the two-pronged track that meandered over the grass and turned behind a boulder. There, out of the wind, was a goat bed, scattered with clumps and strings of dirty white wool. I bent to scoop up handfuls, and Susi picked bits of fleece off a stunted pine tree.

"Aren't you afraid to live by yourself?" I asked, rolling smaller bits of fleece together in a ball. Wool oil glistened on my palms. I rubbed it into the hard ridges of skin where my blisters broke the day before.

Susi shrugged and smiled. She had dimples like me. "What should I be afraid of?" she asked.

"Dark," I said. Everyone I knew was afraid of the dark.

"Yeah," she said, still smiling. "So I light a lamp. Not keeping anyone awake but me."

We moved down the meadow, gathering from shrubs.

"What about . . . strangers?" I said, not wanting to mention the Timber Giant or the Pitch Woman by name.

Susi laughed. "Yeah, I worry about them too. Got myself a big lock very first thing."

We stopped at the edge of the meadow and gazed at Lake Quinault a thousand feet below. It shimmered like an abalone shell against the deep green and silver-gray waves of rain forest. The sight of it pressed at my heart. I had to find a way to stay here, to live here. Canneries and factories were far away. Susi set down her basket and watched me watching our grandmothers' land.

She said, "There are worse things a woman can be than afraid."

I used to love to climb to the top of the headland and look out over the ocean, but after the whale hunt, I couldn't look at the ocean. I wanted to, but I was afraid if I started to look, I'd never look away. I'd turn to stone, forever looking. It sounded like a thing that would happen in one of Grandma's stories.

But in the mountains, the ocean was miles out of sight. The gray, green rain forest set my mind rolling. Why was I still alive? Alone, with no parents and no brothers or sisters of my own? I was the same age as Charlie; why was my luck so different? He was the one obsessed with movies and jazz. Henry was the one who broke the rules of the whale hunt. I had given Ida every dress I'd ever outgrown, and she couldn't share her stupid crayons with me. But they still had each other and both parents. Ten years from now, their children would have aunts and uncles, grandparents and cousins. Not mine.

I slipped my hand into my pocket and touched the abalone shell from my mother's regalia. Touching it helped me think of what Mama would say to me, my secret object, the one I stole before Papa burned all my mother's things. Grandma held me in her lap that day and rocked me, though I was years past rocking.

"This is hard," she whispered. "This goes deep. But

53

he is not wrong to let your mother go so completely. He chooses life with you, and that makes him put death far out of his reach."

I didn't understand. I didn't want to try. But I remembered Grandma's paper-dry cheek next to mine as we sat together while the funeral fires cooled. The next morning, she laid a red leather diary in my lap and a silver fountain pen.

"Your teacher up at the schoolhouse tells me you have a fine hand for lettering. You put that talent to use. Write the names of all your relatives in this book."

I wrote the names and nothing else. It was not beautiful. The pen was shaky in my hand, and the ink dribbled. I wondered if Grandma meant for me to write something more. I wondered why I remembered that diary today, looking down on Lake Quinault from the mountains.

Susi called me over to a patch of wild strawberries. We feasted like bear cubs, and afterward I was ready to sleep like one, but we had baskets of wool to gather and miles to walk before the sun went down. We returned to the wool picking. The large boulders were a favorite scratching post. Cobweb strands of matted wool caught in the crevices. As I wound fibers into a soft ball, I saw, shoulder-high on the rock, a row of circles. They were too regular, too perfectly round to be natural.

"Look at this, Susi," I said.

The circles were as big as a half-dollar and shallow. I ran a finger across the row.

"No one carves in stone," Susi said. "Plenty of men work in bone, antlers, and walrus ivory, but I've never heard of a stone carver."

"It has to be art," I said. "Animals or weather couldn't make this pattern."

I leaned closer to look for a blade or mallet mark. I pressed my palms to the stone. Warmth and life pressed back. I stepped away and checked my hands for some sign of that life pulse. Nothing. I must have been losing my mind.

That night, I had the dream again, the one where my father was calling me, calling me to save him. I ran in pitch darkness looking for him. Only this time, I came close, so close I reached out to take his hand, to pull him up out of death. But I touched stone instead and woke up.

## 6

## *The Museum Man*

The next day, I was full of plans for my wool. I needed to clean and spin it in the summer. Come fall, when we moved back to the longhouse where my mother's loom was waiting, I would learn how to weave. I would teach myself or die trying.

I followed the riverbank upstream, walking on boulders and wading in the shallows. The wool basket rested between my shoulder blades with the tumpline over my forehead. I turned up a steep bank to a clearing that was marked by the skeleton of a lightning-struck tree. It marked the patch of white dirt I needed to sprinkle over my wool to soak up the oil as I pounded it.

Uncle Jeremiah and Uncle Royal were at the far side of the clearing, pacing off the length of a fallen cedar.

Uncle Royal set his palm over the log for a blessing. Uncle Jeremiah did the same. They sang the blessing song over the cedar. I almost cried to hear it. My father used to sing it with Uncle Jeremiah before they made a mask or canoe or totem pole.

Uncle Jeremiah was a better carver than my papa. He could see the canoe inside the tree, the way my father could see a whale under the water. I turned my head to hear the thud-grunt of the adze, the snap-crack and chips of cedar flying. I made my work fit their rhythm. I didn't mean to overhear, but the word "starve" opened my ears wide.

"Don't worry," Uncle Royal said quietly. "We won't let your family starve. Plenty of salmon in the river for everyone this year."

Uncle Jeremiah nodded his thanks but didn't look up.

"You would do the same for us," Uncle Royal said.

I knew it was true, but we had always been the family that gives, not the family that gets. Whatever Uncle Jeremiah said to this, I didn't want to hear it. I tossed clean wool back in with the dirty and hopped from stone to stone across the river. I turned up the north bank to my favorite spot under a willow by the water.

Charlie was already there, fletching arrows. He had a pocketknife in his hand and a pile of duck feathers beside him to split and slide into the notch on the back end of the arrow. He glanced up and swore when he saw me, but it wasn't a very bad swear.

"What are you doing?" I said.

"Grandpa thinks it's time we go back to bow hunting," he said.

"You couldn't hit the broad side of a dairy cow at twenty paces."

"You should talk," he snapped back, whacking me with the end of an arrow. "You going to feed us with that wool you got? Wool soup? Fleece flapjacks?"

I thought about smacking him back, but I remembered my *quelans*. "There aren't any more bullets for Grandpa's hunting rifles, are there?" I said. I dropped my basket of fleece and sat beside him. "Not much sugar or flour either."

Charlie picked up a feather and concentrated on slicing it in half. "Gonna be dark come winter," he said, "with no whale oil to put in our lamps."

"Cold too," I added. "There's only enough flannel left for one winter shirt."

"And we can't put up jam without sugar."

I had been wondering what we'd do without whale oil to trade, but saying it out loud made my mouth go dry.

"What are they going to do about it?" I asked, nodding in the direction of the grown-ups back at camp.

Charlie spent all his time with Grandpa. If something was going on, he would know about it.

Charlie fidgeted. He rolled an arrow between his palms, looking down the shaft to see if it was straight. "We aren't going to starve," he said, setting the work down. "Only a fool could starve in a place as good as this. We'll make up for the whale meat with extra elk or bears."

"We just won't have any money," I said.

Charlie shrugged at the ground. "Happened to some of the Tlingit a while back," he said. "Bunch of sawmills poisoned their river, killed all their salmon. The men and boys went away to work the sawmill and the lumber camps. The women went to some cannery up in Alaska. Only grandparents and babies in that village now. But the workers come home, sometimes."

I had heard gossip about that before, about a Tlingit man who came home from the mill. He had run the flying cut-off saw. Only Indians got that job, maybe sometimes a Chinaman, if he was big. That giant saw flew after him. Cut him off above the elbow. The mill boss could have kept him as a clerk or quartermaster, but no, he sent him home with no salary. Now he was a one-armed fisherman. That family went hungry.

I could tell Charlie was thinking about that story too, by the way he squeezed his elbows in tight to his body.

In the days that followed, I saw Aunt Loula busy

tanning deer and elk hides for the boot and glove maker in town. Grandma twined baskets and little Ida cut sweetgrass for her until her hands were almost as red and chapped as mine. Henry sliced and drilled elk-horn buttons. Uncle Jeremiah carved elk-horn knife handles and letter openers. You could sell all those things in town, but not for very much.

A potlatch messenger would solve our problems, a feast messenger from the Nootka or Kwakiutl or Tsimshian with news of a marriage or an inheritance. We gave away hundreds of pounds of flour, salt, and sugar, many gallons of fish oil, and all the copper we owned. It would be nice to receive next time. It would be fair. They should have known if they sat at our table and took our gifts, they owed us gifts at their own potlatch later.

I took my wool and strips of yellow cedar bark to the lakeshore, where I could spin while I watched the mouth of the river for a messenger. I shaped the clean wool into long pieces and twisted them around a strip of cedar bark as slender and strong as a fish bone. My first tries were awkward and lumpy, but once I got the feel for it, spinning was easier than I remembered. I worked in a steady rhythm, stroking the wool down my thigh with a flat hand to twist two strands, and then reversing the stroke to twist the plies of yarn together.

I watched for the feast messenger every day, but the

long, warm months of *Panklaswhas* and *Panmuulak* passed, and no one came. Would they hold a feast without us, now that the power had gone out of our name?

I fingered Mama's abalone shell. Maybe it was my fault. Maybe Death found Papa because I kept this thing of my mother's. Maybe it drew Death to him. Maybe it's what I deserve for disobeying him, disobeying and lying.


Susi saved me that summer. It was a good year for berries, so every weekend when the post office was closed, she drove up to pick, sort, pound, and dry berries with me by the shore of the lake. And when I wanted to talk, she was full of news from all up and down the coast. She could sing songs straight from the radio. But when I didn't want to talk, she worked by my side, bumping my arm from time to time to draw me away from my thoughts.

One day, she stepped out of her car with a newspaper for Uncle Jeremiah and a letter for Grandpa. He didn't ask, but I knew to read it aloud, translating to Makah as I went. Uncle Jeremiah heard me read and found a reason to bring the paddle he was carving near. Aunt Loula didn't even pretend to be working. Henry and Charlie stayed put, but they listened without looking.

The letter was from some man called Arthur Glen, from some place he called the Art Institute.

15 August 1923

From:
Mr. Arthur Glen
The Art Institute
New York City

To:
Mr. Simon Carver
Ozette, Washington State

Dear Sir:

I am an avid collector of the
artifacts of the Pacific Tribes.
I have a special interest in carved
totem poles and masks. I have heard
the reputation of your family,
and I am eager to visit and study
you.

I have a stipend from the Art
Institute to add to their excellent
and world-renowned collection.
I will be arriving on the tenth
of October.

Respectfully yours,
Mr. Arthur Glen

"Another collector," Uncle Jeremiah said. "We haven't seen one in these parts for a dozen years."

"More totem poles, bah! How can they want more? There are more poles in New York and Chicago than there are in the whole state of Washington," Grandpa said.

"I wonder which kind of collector he will be," Uncle Jeremiah said.

"Well, if he's the grave-robbing kind, we'll do this with him," Grandpa said, and he crushed a mussel shell in his bare hand. "But more likely he's a pole and mask man."

"Or maybe he's the type to want the full story with all the 'savage' embellishments," Henry said.

Susi took the envelope from my hand and checked the address. She turned to Henry. "Isn't the Art Institute in Chicago? This letter is from New York."

"We've sold to Chicago before, but it wasn't the art museum. Have you ever heard of this collector?" Henry gave Susi a look, and I could tell they were both suspicious.

"I could ask around," Susi said.

Grandpa brushed aside their worries. "White people are always moving things. We'll ask him his references when he comes."

"Some of them want baskets," Aunt Loula piped up.

"And I've heard of one who would bring you a plant and pay you to tell its name and its use."

"The trouble is, will he be the type to buy old things, the more battered the better, or will he want fresh carvings with new paint?" Grandpa paced a few steps from his carving work and back.

"It's easy enough to make old carving." Uncle Jeremiah laughed. "Rub on some sand, knock off a few corners, soak it for a day, and leave it in the sun."

"We have old masks to sell," Grandpa said abruptly. "We will spend our time on new work."

I could not believe what I was hearing. They would let a stranger come in and buy things, ceremonial things? Did we really have so little money that we would consider it? I remembered my father's Raven mask and cape.

"What if he doesn't want to buy our things?" I blurted out. "What if he's a liar or a common thief? We don't know anything about this man."

"He's one man," Grandpa said. "If he treats us badly, we'll send him away. Don't worry, Pearl, a guest in our own house won't steal from us."

I brought out the paper box. Grandpa selected a thin sheet, sharpened a pen, and dipped it in ink for me. I translated his words in my best hand.

*2 September 1923*

*From:*
*Simon Carver*
*Ozette, Washington State*

*To:*
*Mr. Arthur Glen*
*The Art Institute*
*New York City*

*Dear Sir:*
*You are welcome to come to our village in October of this year to study our ways and bargain for our carving. You will find no travelers' lodging at my village. Please be a guest in my home. Come to the Kalaloch Post Office. We will bring you the rest of the way.*
*Respectfully yours,*
*Simon Carver*

Grandpa examined my writing. He took heavy paper from the box. He folded an envelope and sealed the letter inside with flour paste. Henry frowned, and Charlie looked worried, but they would not cross Grandpa's word. They drifted back to their own work and I was alone with him.

"What does that museum man really want, Grandpa?" I asked. "Washington is a long way to come."

"This Arthur Glen is looking to take from us," Grandpa said. "He'll call it buying or collecting or research. He will have heard from other museum men the reputation of the mask makers in our family, the Bear mask with the full skin, the Whale that turns into a man. He will want those."

"But what for?" I pressed, thinking of my father's chest of masks.

"For power, Pearl. Why else would a nation keep a treasure house? Think how it is when a man holds a potlatch. All his wealth arrayed, and he gives it away. His friends think, this powerful man is my ally. I will do anything for him. His enemies think, this is only what he shows, what he can afford to give away. What powers does he have that I don't see? Do you understand how it is, Pearl?" Grandpa leaned toward me now with his hands on my shoulders.

"Your friends are stronger, your rivals weaker, and not a drop of blood is shed. It's a weak nation that chooses killing."

It was on the tip of my tongue to say, why should we give him or even sell him what gives us power? But

I noticed Grandpa's arm was thinner than it used to be under his green-and-blue calico work shirt, and there were streaks of gray in his short black hair that were not there a summer ago.

I slipped my hand into Grandpa's and gave it a quick squeeze. "Don't worry. I'll make your guest welcome, the way my mama would have."

As I walked up to the summer lodge, I stroked Mama's abalone shell in my pocket. Would she have made a collector welcome? I wondered.

Susi was there unrolling a blanket on the table. There was a green cotton dress inside. Susi gave it a shake.

"I haven't worn this in years," she said. "Your mother picked out the fabric for me. She would want you to have it."

I took the dress, relieved that Susi had found a way to make it look as if I was obeying my mother and not as if I was taking charity.

"What did Uncle Jeremiah want with a newspaper?" I asked once the dress was folded and set aside. Susi glanced around the room for listeners. Ida had taken the maddening habit of following me everywhere that summer. I heard her screaming and splashing in the lake with Charlie. Susi turned to me looking grim.

"He hasn't said, but I know that the Friday paper has advertisements for lumberjacks and mill hands, some local work and lots of ads for Alaska and Montana. Loula will be looking at the canneries."

"Do girls work in canneries?" I interrupted. "I mean, girls my age."

Susi put a hand on my shoulder. "Look at you, you're as tall as a grown woman. Taller than some. They would never ask your age."

"What about Charlie?" I asked. "Charlie's too little for lumberjacking."

"I've heard the mining companies are looking for boys his age."

We could hear Charlie laughing and splashing Ida. Susi was about to cry.

"It's not settled, is it?" I asked, to comfort me as much as her. "We've worked hard all summer and there is leather, buttons, baskets." I paused. All that work, there must be more than that to sell, but most of our efforts had gone into smoking and drying food for the winter.

"What we need," Susi said, dabbing her eyes at the corner, "is something white people need, like whale oil for their machines. Or something they think they need, like jazz or rouge."

She walked to where the newspaper sat on the table. The front page showed a fancy man and lady aboard a steamship. Susi flipped a few pages in, where another picture showed a couple eating at a San Francisco restaurant. Susi tapped the page.

"Oysters," she said firmly. "Oysters Rockefeller and Manhattan clam chowder. It's all the rage in San Francisco. The showy types buy it at five dollars a plate."

I calculated prices in my head. Aunt Loula and Grandma and I always took a couple dozen pounds of shellfish in the fall, but if the men worked too, we'd have a hundred pounds—easy.

"Fresh is the thing," I pointed out. "Unless we're going to smoke them, we want to sell the day after we catch."

Susi turned to the shipping schedule on the back page. "A steamer leaves from Aberdeen next week. If we could get the clams there alive, they'd put them on ice."

I thought over the times I'd dug clams. Usually, we only took as many as we could smoke the next day, but once we gathered extra and kept them fresh in a box full of seawater. I looked out the door at the lake. The uncles were putting the finishing touches on their canoe. It was a beauty, a ten-seater with plenty of room for cargo.

"Susi, do you think we could put my little fish canoe inside that one and still have room to paddle? We could keep two hundred pounds of oysters and clams fresh in a canoe full of water."

"Do you think the men will agree to dig clams?" Susi asked. "What would your dad say?"

I tapped over the outside of my dress pocket looking for something—my father's sharpening stone, a gold button from his Russian Navy coat, the baby spoon he carved for me. Nothing was there. I couldn't think of what he would say to me. I knew what Uncle Jeremiah would say, though. He was Grandpa's twin in keeping the old ways. This was not going to be easy.

I paced a few laps around the floor and swallowed back the lump in my throat. "If my father was alive," I said, "we would have our whale and not be in this trouble. It's my choice now, and I choose not to be poor. I choose to stay here, to live on my land."

# 7

## *The Clam Tide*

It wasn't easy to tell them my plan for gathering shell-fish, not even with Susi beside me holding the facts: $3 a pound, Steamship *Liberty,* Slip 29, Aberdeen. Ida stared at me openmouthed, as if I had claimed whales could fly. Charlie matched his frown to Grandpa's, shaking his head and puffing out his belly.

But Henry walked to my side, put a hand on my shoulder, and said, "I'll help."

His father laid into him first. "Never been done! You're old enough to take a wife, son. What will she think if you do her work?"

"She'll think I'm not a whaler anymore. These are new times; I'll take any work that helps my family."

His words bit like frost. It was plain they had argued

this matter before. Had I kicked the pebble that started a landslide?

Henry and Uncle Jeremiah stepped closer with their heads up and fists tight, the way men do before boxing. Grandpa stepped between them with a hand on each chest. I saw him gathering up words to pass judgment.

Grandma beat him to it. "I'll need your help with the bargaining, Simon," she said. "You know how a white man hates to talk money with a woman, especially an Indian woman. We'll get a better price if you make the deal."

Grandpa paused to collect a new set of arguments.

Aunt Loula took the hint and added a helping of sugar to her voice. "It's a long way to paddle, Aberdeen."

Uncle Jeremiah turned his scowl from his son to his wife. "You'll not go without a proven navigator along." He announced it as though the trip had been his idea from the start. "Our canoe is finished. It should have a first voyage."

"We'll wait two days for a better tide," Grandpa added with a note of finality. "And I hear from old McCreedy who hears from the Tulalip who trade with the Skokomish in Puget Sound that someone sank a boat over the Hood Canal oyster beds. Oil and dead fish everywhere. Nobody's shipping oysters out of the sound this year. We'll get better than three dollars a pound."

He gave a satisfied huff and surveyed his family.

"Show me a man with a boatload of ice, and I'll show you a man in a hurry to make a sale."

Ida's mouth was open so wide a squirrel could have crawled in and made a nest.

Charlie gave a short laugh of relief and said, "I'll dig clams and stay in school this winter. Anything's better than going down in a mine."

So the clam digging was settled. Susi gave my hand a squeeze. Grandma kissed my cheek, and then gave me a long look as if she were seeing me for the first time.

When the tide was right, we took our canoes down the Quinault River and out to the ocean. We followed the coast south to the beach just past Taholah and made camp.

At dawn, the clam beach was cold, flat, and yards wider than usual with the minus tide. There were star prints in the sand from gulls and pelicans and the little hands of a raccoon along the edge of a shallow creek that emptied into the ocean. I walked slowly. The wet sand reflected the sky, and clouds rushed dizzy under my feet. I searched for bubbles that stood up enough to break the reflection. When I saw one, I dug as fast as I could with the stick to get the clam before it burrowed out of reach. It was tricky to get one. Whenever I was able to flip one out of its hole, I was tempted to shout with satisfaction like Ida did.

My family was spread out over two or three acres, walking, digging, and carrying clams to boxes full of seawater. Three boxes were filled by midmorning. My hands were rough from sand and stiff from cold, but it was worth it. I loved all of us working together. In the rain. Here. On our own land. I thought of all the generations before me who had come to this place and collected this food. Before Spanish pirates and Russian traders and French trappers and American settlers, there was only my family, my people, and all the treasures of the ocean were ours to take.

For the flash of a moment, I saw a trail of children following Charlie, and five more clustered around Ida— their children, I was sure of it. I spun to look behind me. There was a crowd of footprints, long and little. One wave later, and there was nothing but smooth sand. My heart beat faster. It was the flicker of certainty I had secretly been praying for. I would not be alone forever. Someday I would have a family of my own.

The next morning, we made ready for our trip to town. Aunt Loula and Ida wanted to take the truck, but we could empty it completely and there still wouldn't be enough room for the clams and oysters. And the road was so bumpy, we'd have to pack them up dry. They'd die on the way into town. The canoe would carry the clams in water and all of us together. The men packed rope around the fish canoe and its load of clams to keep it from tipping. I smoothed the pleats of my town skirt and turned up the sleeves of my blouse for the paddling. Ida hopped about waiting to put the bundle of deerskins in the canoe. Aunt Loula put lunches in a basket.

We took our places, and Uncle Jeremiah launched us. Grandpa sat across from Charlie and taught him navigation. They read the weather first, then the currents. Charlie named each sea stack, headland, and freshwater creek in Makah, in Quinault, and in English if they bothered to name it. Grandpa explained how to keep track of time on the water and how to judge a storm. I took in all that information and set it firmly in my memory, but I was careful not to show my interest. It was enough that Grandpa agreed to men digging clams. Even I knew better than to propose women navigators.

When the fog lifted, it was a perfect fall day, cool wind and not a cloud for miles. Uncle Jeremiah put up the mast and set the sail. We moved with good speed south to Aberdeen.

Now that I could relax, I couldn't help thinking how deep the water was beneath me and how dark and cold. I couldn't help thinking, is he down there? The memory of that nightmare of looking for my father and trying to follow his voice made me shiver. To distract myself, I took a handful of pebbles from my pocket. I had been saving this trick to show Ida—how to call porpoises up from the deep.

"Look!" I said, and tossed the pebbles over the water. I waited a few minutes and tossed again. Ida looked, but she didn't have the patience to wait.

"Look there," Uncle Jeremiah said, pointing to a slight change in the ripples.

A porpoise burst out of the water, leaping in a rainbow arch. Three more and then another lifted their heads above the water. Ida gasped and clapped.

Grandma called, "*Nah-gwee-nau,*" and tossed bits of pilot bread. The porpoises snapped up the food. It was impossible not to laugh at their chubby, frowning faces.

All at once they dove, and my mind went down with them. What if he's alive down there, I thought, hidden away or kept prisoner in the deep houses of the whales? What if he's waiting for some sign or gift or sacrifice?

My heart raced, and I knew what I had to do. I took the piece of shell, my mother's abalone from her button blanket, and I cradled it in my hand. I glanced around at my family. All of them were looking at the water, lost in thought. Even Uncle Jeremiah seemed not to steer.

I held the smooth, flat shell to my cheek. It curved

just enough to perfectly cup my face. Then, when no one was looking, I let it go. For a minute, I could see it shine like the moon underwater, and then it was lost in darkness. As my mother's last thing dropped away, I felt my body grow lighter, so much that I gripped the edge of the boat to keep from floating up over the mast. My head spun, and I squeezed my eyes shut. From far off, I heard Charlie sing. It was a child's paddle song, and Charlie sang it pure and clear. There was no weight of age in his voice. I closed my eyes tighter and clung to that song.

We camped that night right outside of town. The next morning we were on the water at sunup. We turned into Grays Harbor and sailed up the bay to Aberdeen. We passed fishing trawlers and dories stacked with crab pots. There was a clatter of metalwork from the shipyards and the deep voices of longshoremen. A cloud of smoke poured from the railroad yard. We could smell tar and raw logs. A pilot recognized the design of our canoe with the head of Raven carved on the prow. He rang his bell and hailed us from the pilothouse. We lifted our paddles to our old trading partner.

When we pulled alongside the steamship *Liberty*, a redheaded man with tan spots on his face climbed down a pilot's ladder and stepped into our canoe. He shook hands with the men and made a bow to the women that set our boat rocking.

Grandpa smiled at Uncle Jeremiah and said, *"Cheechako."* Newcomer.

*"Skookum Cheechako* to you, Simon Carver," the red-headed man answered. "You may not know O'Neil, but O'Neil knows of you. Newcomer indeed; I bought oil off your nephew Frank in Neah Bay three years ago and halibut from your cousin Solomon Jackson last month."

"And you'll buy clams from me today, Red O'Neil," Grandpa answered back faster than I had ever heard him talk. "You won't find better—not this year."

"Is that a fact." Red smiled. He plunged a hand into our catch uninvited, stirring through the shellfish all the way to the bottom.

"Alive-o. Well done, ma'am." He bowed to Grandma and Aunt Loula again, who laughed openly at his extravagant manners. Red fished out a pair of clams and flipped them open with a knife. He poked and sniffed and swallowed.

"Dollar fifty a pound and not a copper more," Red announced.

"Six dollars or I'll heave you overboard," Grandpa answered.

"Ooh, you're a filthy pirate, you are. I'll clap you in irons, but not before I offer a dollar eighty-five."

"You're a man with an empty hold," Grandpa said. He pointed to the load waterline. "I'll take six dollars firm."

Insults and prices volleyed back and forth. It was better to watch than baseball. On cue, Grandma chanted a Quinault lullaby that Grandpa claimed was an ancient Indian curse. O'Neil responded by assigning us all to the deepest circle of hell. When it was over, we settled on $4.10 a pound. Red wrote it out in showy penmanship on the bill of sale. He passed out peppermints to Ida and me and called Grandpa a few more profanities, and we went to the scales to weigh and collect pay.

# 8

## *A Day in Town*

We walked up from the harbor and into town. Each time we came, Aberdeen was larger. Houses sprang up along the edges of the business district like rings of mushrooms. A new three-level dormitory stood between the lumberyard and the railroad terminal. Charlie lingered by the door of every diner and pool hall with ragtime piano playing.

We stopped at the cobbler shops first. Uncle Jeremiah did the bargaining, but luck was against us. A new dairyman up in the hills had a contract with every boot maker in town. We finally found a glover to buy our deerskins, but he paid half of what we got the year before.

Still, we had made a good profit on our shellfish. There would be enough money for clothes and winter groceries. Maybe we wouldn't need to sell ceremonial things when the museum man came to visit. I held my head up and perused the shop windows as if I had the power to buy anything they might have for show. A block before the department store, we passed the curio shop, and by unspoken agreement the entire family stopped. Grandma and Aunt Loula looked over the baskets for sale.

"Dora's work," Grandma said, pointing to an especially fine basket with a geometric pattern in brown and green, "from Neah Bay."

"This is Annabelle's favorite weave," Aunt Loula said of another.

A cowbell jangled as the shop door opened. An Indian woman, older than Aunt Loula and younger than Grandma, stepped out onto the street. She had an empty cloth sack under her arm and a small slip of paper in her hand. I didn't recognize her, but Grandma seemed to know her well. Grandma greeted the woman in Makah, and she answered back in a language that was similar to ours but enough different that I couldn't translate. It was probably basket chat anyway.

Grandpa and Uncle Jeremiah frowned over a Hamatsa mask displayed prominently in the window. It belonged to such a scary story, I didn't want to look at it, but Grandpa was upset because it was a secret society mask. A man was supposed to guard it with all his honor and take it out only for the winter ceremonies.

81

"I think it belongs to the Raymond Sook outfit," Henry said quietly.

I took a step closer to hear but pretended to be looking at the baskets on the bottom shelf of the store window.

"Did you hear about him?" Uncle Jeremiah said, still frowning. "Terrible fall."

"He was a topper for that logging company out of Hoquiam," Henry said. "Came down off the crown of a fir he was topping. Maybe a hundred feet. He hasn't walked in a year."

Grandpa turned to Uncle Jeremiah when he heard this, as though he had something to say, maybe something to whisper to him. But Uncle Jeremiah turned away, fixing his eyes to some empty spot down the street. He wouldn't even look at his father. It was such a little thing. I wouldn't have noticed if I hadn't been standing right beside them, but I could tell they had been fighting, the way Henry was fighting with Uncle Jeremiah over helping with the clams. Henry paused a moment longer, cleared his throat, and went on. "There's only a brother and a sister left to look after Raymond and all those children and the grandparents too. They'll suffer this winter if he doesn't sell it."

"He'd get a better price in Seattle," Uncle Jeremiah said.

Two hundred dollars seemed an amazing price to me,

but shopkeepers were a strange bunch. They didn't care how long it took you to make a thing or how famous your family was for carving or weaving. They wanted a thing because some other shopkeeper had one or maybe because there was a nearly identical mask at the World's Fair. I took a closer look and saw, behind the mask, a woven blanket and a price card that said AUTHENTIC INDIAN BLANKET, HAND-WOVEN, $200.

I couldn't believe it, a blanket worth as much as a man's mask! And it wasn't even a Chilkat blanket, with the perfect circles and patterns that show the faces of Bear or Raven. It was a plain Salish blanket with broad stripes in three colors. It was finely woven, probably one of the older dog wool blankets, but still, if I could learn to weave, I'd have blankets worth twice as much. It wouldn't matter if no chief or famous house could give me a commission. I'd sell to white collectors and museums. The baskets were pathetic by comparison—two dollars, five at the very most for the big ones. The shopkeeper didn't set a higher price for Dora's or Annabelle's work, even though it was better than anything else in the store.

That's it, I promised myself. I'll weave, and then I'll have enough money to buy my own wool and pearl buttons for a button blanket, enough money to stay on my own land. As we moved on down the street, I remembered the design my father had drawn for me. I figured yards of wool in red and black and imagined how I would decorate the borders. Maybe I would make an outline of waves to represent the dreams of my father, to show that I was a daughter of whalers.

The department store was a block farther on. The men headed downstairs for tools and hardware. The women skipped the ready-made clothes and church hats on the main floor and went up the broad wooden staircase for dry goods. Aunt Loula picked out bolts of flannel and broadcloth for shirts, hard canvas for men's work pants, and plain muslin for underthings. My fingers ached at the thought of all that sewing.

Ida and I matched threads at the ribbon counter. There were two shopgirls there; one was winding new ribbon onto spools, and the other stood at the cutting table, folding and marking remnants. They carried on an easy conversation about the latest Valentino movie and the cut of fall blouses. They were as relaxed with each other as sisters, and I watched them out of the corner of my eye. When I spoke with Anita or Dorothy, we sometimes talked about movies or a book we had read at school, but we never got around to ribbon color or the fashion of ready-made clothes.

The ribbon winder had sea-green eyes and hair as yellow as a fall leaf. She wore it in one thick braid that fell over her shoulder. She took one color of ribbon after another and laid it on her shoulder so her friend could admire the effect.

"Baby blue, oh, I don't know," she said.

"Blue goes with blond," the other insisted. "It says so right in the *Ladies Home Journal.*"

"But every Sonja from Little Sweden will be wearing blue," the ribbon girl said. "How about red, scarlet red!"

The friend burst out laughing. "As if Mrs. Hardy would let you out her door in red. 'I have a reputation to keep up, young lady, even if you don't!' I bet she was a prison matron before she ran our boardinghouse."

I liked the remnant folder better. She had jet-black hair done up in a twist, brown eyes, and shoulders as broad as mine. She never wasted a motion in folding and labeling her yard goods.

"Lavender, that's what you want," the black-haired girl went on. "Soft like blue, but distinctive. Not that you've got a penny to spare for ribbon, what with stopping at the chocolate shop every other day."

"Oh, you can afford to be virtuous." The ribbon girl pouted. "You already have a beau to buy you chocolates."

I could be that brown-eyed shopgirl. Any fool could stand at a counter, dust goods, and make change. I could move to town. The schoolmaster always said we should. I could get a proper job and live with other girls my age and spend my days indoors in a clean skirt and blouse thinking of nothing more difficult than what movie to watch and who to dance with at the Woodchoppers' Ball.

I tried to catch the shopgirl's eye to see if she would smile at me, but she didn't give Ida and me a glance. When Aunt Loula finally came to the cutting table with a dozen bolts of cloth, an older woman appeared from a back room to do the cutting and tallying up.

Our next stop was the grocer. Grandma shooed me and Ida off to the city park, while they ordered their cases and barrels. Ida and I picked up a game of kickball with some town girls. The grown-ups met us an hour later, and we ate our lunch under the red-gold maple trees. Afterward, we walked to the Victory Movie Parlor. Grandpa was all smiles.

"Gifts for hardworking grandchildren," he said. "Littlest first."

Ida got knitting needles and a skein of thick pink yarn. I could hear her crow already. With ten minutes' practice, she would be better at knitting than I was.

Charlie got a Hohner harmonica and immediately picked out a jazzy tune he had heard that afternoon.

"I chose these for you," Grandma said, with an arm around my shoulder. She opened her hand to show five pencils and a Swiss folding knife. I hid my disappointment behind a smile.

"Pencils, thanks," I said. "I guess you noticed, I haven't been keeping my diary."

Grandma shrugged. "Ink is tricky," she said.

I opened the knife and worked on a pencil point. The shavings released a faint cedar smell.

Grandma lifted my chin. "When you write a word down, you own that word forever," she said.

The Victory was the fanciest place in town. It was a glittering palace on the outside, with electric lights and mirrors. Inside, it had green carpeting with gold swirls and a velvet curtain with thick gold fringe. The seats had cushions, and the lamps had sparkling diamonds. I wouldn't have been surprised to find the Queen of Sheba sitting right up in the front row.

I felt like royalty walking down the center aisle. We took seats in the middle row, and Ida pestered me to death with questions about the movie stars on painted posters along the side walls. It was Charlie Chaplin that afternoon, with a musical interlude from the piano player before the show and at intermission. We had only been seated a moment when a well-dressed woman stood up with a sniff of disdain. She clutched her two children close and pushed past our chairs. She made a big show of sitting as far from us as possible.

There was a moment's pause while the rest of the theatergoers got over the need to stare at us. Charlie leaned toward Henry, batted his eyelashes, and pretended to point and gossip about some scandalous thing. Aunt Loula smiled, and Grandma smacked Charlie on the arm but not very hard. Then Charlie stood up and walked in front of our chairs, doing the white-woman wag you see sometimes in the well-dressed ladies in town. Ida and Henry laughed out loud. Grandma hid her smile behind a handkerchief, and Grandpa resorted to a fit of coughing.

The theater filled for the matinee, all but the seats nearest us. People laughed and chatted with their neighbors. Men argued the board-foot price of lumber. Ladies admired each other's hats and gossiped over the skirt length of certain unchaperoned girls at the theater. I had always loved the busy variety of people at the movies. I loved feeling as if I were a part of the story told on the screen and sharing it with people who seemed so different but laughed at all the same things I did. I could see Ida drinking it all in, but for the first time I saw what she didn't. No one spoke to us. No one even looked in our direction. We were dressed as well as all but the fanciest moviegoers. We had paid the same cash price for a ticket, but their silent indifference said you don't belong here, as clear as shouting. Charlie Chaplin was as funny as ever, but this time I didn't laugh.

I bet no one scorned those shopgirls. I bet they could sit wherever they chose in theaters, churches, and cafés. I was no darker than the black-haired girl. I did not look so foreign as a Chinaman, and I spoke better English than any off-the-boat immigrant working man. I was so angry I wanted to spit on that high-and-mighty woman. But what if she was the boardinghouse matron? What if she did the hiring at the department store? I would have to hide my Indian life if I wanted to live in town. I would have to make up a story about my circumstances. I would fashion myself a character like the young women in the penny dreadful novels the older girls passed around at school, a virtuous girl who hit hard times and had to make a living on nothing but her own determination.

I could do it if I wanted to. I could put on a white woman's clothes and high voice and little steps. But then I would never be able to sing or dance in my own language, never be able to bring a visitor or a token from home to my boardinghouse in town. I weighed it against my life on the reservation with all its work and worry, and both seemed too heavy to bear.

Uncle Jeremiah and I paddled the small canoe home that evening since it was empty of clams. Daylight held until we reached the mouth of Grays Harbor, and after a break for a meal, the rising moon gave us light to travel by.

The little canoe held the lighter goods—cloth, needles,

thread, soap, two pairs of spike-soled logger boots, and two pairs of long rubber cannery-worker gloves. I looked at them, and Uncle Jeremiah saw me look. We said nothing for more than a mile.

"We cannot always count on four dollars a pound for clams," he said. "Next year, something else will be fashionable. Next year, the Hood Canal beaches will be clean and more shellfish will be on the market. We won't have to go away to find work this winter, but next year . . ." Uncle Jeremiah went quiet, and we both watched the fall constellations rise from the horizon to point our way.

"Next year, we must be ready for anything," he said.

"But it's so far away," I said. "We would only see each other every other month. Maybe less. What about Grandma and Grandpa? They couldn't possibly go work in a factory. Ida's too little. Would we leave her behind with nobody but Grandma and Grandpa to take care of her?"

I was glad Uncle Jeremiah sat behind me in the canoe where he couldn't see my face. I hated sharing a room with Ida, but the idea of her sleeping all alone made my heart sink. It wasn't natural for a child to sleep in a room alone.

"Maybe this museum man who comes next week will have carving work for us," Uncle Jeremiah said. "We don't have to go away yet, but we can't stay on land that won't support us either."

Maybe he'll be a bone hunter and dig up graves, I thought, but I didn't say it because Uncle Jeremiah sounded so sad. He was right. I knew he was right, but I wanted to know what my mother would say. I reached for my pocket and the abalone shell I had always kept there. But I had nothing of my mother's now, and I'd never felt more empty.

# 9

## *At the Loom*

When we arrived home, I was ready to put all my energy into weaving, but Aunt Loula was making winter shirts and wanted me to do buttons and hems, and there were always people to feed. More frustrating than all the chores put together was Ida following me everywhere, demanding another round of the bone game or hounding me to read her a chapter in her tattered copy of *The Wizard of Oz*. Whenever I had a moment to spare, I was out the door gathering what I needed to make dye for my wool. I collected iron nails from the driftwood and fresh hemlock bark from the forest for the black dye. I set an old copper pot full of pee out to age for the second dye bath.

Grandma did not care to see me working the wool. I

could tell by the way she followed me on my gathering, pretending she needed bark for medicine or maidenhair ferns for her baskets. One day, when I was inside dipping skeins of wool into the first bath of black dye, she sat on the bench nearby. I noticed that her hands were more wrinkled than last year. She took a white skein of yarn in her calloused hands, held it up to the lamplight to examine the twist, and gave it a nod of approval.

"When your mother first passed from us," Grandma said slowly, "I thought of the loom as a thing belonging to her mother and to her sisters up north. We sent word that they were welcome to take your mother's loom and the blanket she had begun."

I was ready to protest for my right to my mother's loom, but something in my grandmother's defeated look made me hold my thought and keep peace with her.

"Your mother's people sent us word that they would come and bring the loom back to their village, and they would bring you with it, so that you could learn the language and stories of your mother's people."

"What?"

I had heard plenty of stories about my mother's people when I was little but not this one. I stopped stirring the wool in the dye pot and out of habit reached for the abalone shell that was no longer in my pocket.

"Yes, your mother came from powerful people, the

Tlingit, up north. She was the pride of her family, and they were shocked to see her choose a southern husband. But your father"—and here Grandma lifted her chin and put pride in her voice—"your father made a fortune in whale oil as a young man, and he had the Raven stories. There was none but him with the right to dance and sing the entire cycle of Raven stories. It took a whole week of evening ceremonies to dance them through from the first to the last. And it didn't hurt that he was as handsome as the devil and knew how to make a girl laugh."

I left my wool in the dye pot and sat beside Grandma on the bench. This was a story I hadn't heard before.

"You mean it wasn't an arrangement between fathers?" Grandpa took pains, whenever the subject came up, to tell me he would be picking my husband from among men of a certain station.

Grandma laughed and squeezed my arm. "The fathers set the marriage terms, you can be sure of that, but your parents loved each other." She paused and turned away from me. "The last five years would have been easier for your father if they had not."

That was true enough. After my mother died, Papa was not a handsome man, and he spent little effort making me laugh. I went back to my dye pot to stir and lift the wool to check the depth of color.

"Why didn't I go to my mother's people?"

"Your father wouldn't hear of it," Grandma said. "He just couldn't let you go. There were some who said he should take a new wife, one who would give him sons." She glanced rather sternly in the direction of Grandpa's workbench. "But he would have no part of that. So here you are."

Grandma stood up and moved beside me. She held the lamp close so I could check the color of my wool against the black that was already woven into the blanket. It was hard to tell if I had it right, matching wet yarn to dry.

"I'm not sorry he kept you here," she said. "I would have missed my Pearl. But you have lost something none of us can replace."

I busied myself stirring another batch of wool into the pot.

"Maybe you wish we had chosen differently," she added.

My mother's people—they would know how to weave. Maybe I had another grandmother or a whole new set of aunts. I could visit them, and they would help me learn. I smiled and turned to her.

"Do they still want me?"

"We have been looking for them," Grandma said. "People don't travel the way they used to. So many people work for wages now. You can't get a month off to paddle to Alaska. Some villages plain don't have enough manpower to move a seagoing canoe. Messengers are not so easy to send. But the basket maker we met in town, the one at the curio shop, she is from Vancouver Island."

I nodded, remembering. She spoke Nootka—similar to Makah, but not close enough for me to understand easily.

"Her brothers had been up north, and they went to your mother's village. It was empty. Nothing but house frames and frogs left."

"Completely empty?"

Grandma nodded.

"Was it the influenza?" I couldn't bear to think it.

"No, Pearl, there were no unburied bodies. Nothing to show a battle either. Might be they moved to another village or a town, maybe a city—Ketchikan is not so far, or Sitka."

"They're gone? How could they be gone?" I said, my anger growing. "They can't just disappear."

"We'll find them," Grandma said firmly. "But it will take time, Pearl, maybe a very long time. Sometimes the missionaries write down where people move. Maybe they joined a village just a few miles away."

"So there really is no one to teach me to weave?"

Grandma bowed her head and did not answer.

"Fine," I snapped. "I don't need a teacher." I paced a few times from the dye pot to the loom. "I sat beside Mama and watched all the time when she wove. I'll remember how to do it. I'll figure it out by myself."

A week passed. Fall rain raised the rivers, and the Silvers started to spawn up the Quinault River. My wool was dyed deep black, blue-green, and yellow. I sat at the tall loom against the wall in a dim corner of the longhouse. The half-finished face of Bear gazed back at me.

I unwound an arm's length of black wool and worked it over and under to fill in the line below the eye. I concentrated on holding my hands exactly the way Mama had. I tried to remember what she'd said about tension and forming a curved line. Doubt sat in my stomach like bad fish, but I kept working. I unwove the last row my mother worked to check how it was done, but even with the bends and twists pressed into the yarn I couldn't reweave it right, not exactly right. My row was bumpy and rose above the smooth skin of my mother's weaving like a scar. I didn't know how to fix it. Mama never said a lot about her weaving. When she did say something, it wasn't very helpful.

When she was pregnant with my baby sister, she said, "Hold the baby right, and she stops crying. Hold the warp yarns right, and the weaving comes out smooth."

Or she would point to a mistake before she fixed it and say, "Never leave uneven work in a blanket. And never leave an argument standing with your husband. Honor his work as much as you honor your own."

Why had she never said exactly how to weave? I kicked at the base that held up the loom crossbar to make myself remember. I tugged on each end of the yarn to make the row even, but it didn't smooth out the bumpy stitches in the middle. I slid my fingers between the vertical warp threads and pressed my row tight to the row above.

It still didn't look better. It looked worse. I yanked my yarn out of the warp threads, hopped off the weaving bench, and paced.

All I could remember was how natural it had looked when my mother did it, how easy. I remembered how her hands moved steadily in pace with the song she sang. Why didn't I look closer when she was alive? Why didn't I ask more questions?

Aunt Loula called me to lunch and called me again, and then she steered me to the table, two hands on my shoulders, and sat me down. I could not smell the soup. It had no taste. It wouldn't go down. I paddled my spoon around in the bowl when Grandpa took notice, but my throat was closed.

What if I couldn't remember my father's dances either? What if I could only see how beautiful they were and how easy he'd made it look to dance like Raven? What if my sons received the masks and never learned to dance?

I thought of the footprints of my descendants on the beach. Would those feet ever dance, or would they trudge after me to factories and lumber camps and cities far from home? The weight of them following me burned. I hopped up and paced the room to outrun them, heart racing and the touch of flame on my skin.

# 10

## *A Visit with Susi*

I paced the floor, numb, not seeing or hearing, only obeying the urge to keep moving the way an animal keeps moving even in a cage. It was long enough to scare Aunt Loula. Long enough to make Ida cry. Long enough for Henry and Charlie to move the loom out of sight. That night Grandma, Grandpa, and Uncle Jeremiah made hours of quiet talk by the fire. They decided I needed a change.

Everything was set the next day. Grandpa packed a good knife and wool blankets. Aunt Loula and Uncle Jeremiah saw to the food. Grandma wrapped herbs in bundles for sore throat, cough, pain, and rest. Henry gave me a long wool army coat and fur mitts. Ida slipped my diary and a pencil in the basket with my change of clothes.

"You can have any crayon of mine that you want to borrow," she said proudly. "If it is green or blue or purple."

I didn't care about those stupid crayons, but Aunt Loula smiled, proud of Ida's generosity, so I had to take one of each and say thank you. When the good-byes were done, I set off in the fish canoe that Grandma passed down to me. It was just me and the waves for the whole day it would take me to paddle to Susi's post office in Kalaloch. I dug the paddle into the water and named each sea stack and headland I passed in Quinault and Makah and English. The weather, current, and tide were a book I could read, just as my father had. I stopped twice to rest on beaches with drinking water. The burning weight I felt at home was already behind me.

Late that afternoon, I came to the door with the bright brass plaque: MISS SUSANNA JAMES, POSTMISTRESS. Susi was not expecting me, but when she opened her door, I smelled fresh mussels and fry bread, and there was enough for two. Aunt Susi lived in one long, low-ceilinged room over the post office. There was a glass window at each end and a squat black cookstove in the middle. I loved the pin-neatness of the room: a broom in one corner, clothes pegs on the wall, and one open cupboard that held four books and three dishes.

Susi carried a shipping crate upstairs for my chair. She heaped a generous plate for me and opened a pot of huckleberry jam on the table. We began the meal with the required questions about family health, the weather, and the strength of the fall salmon runs. Susi didn't ask why I came, and I wasn't sure what to tell her about those feet following mine and wanting to do right by folks who haven't been born yet. It sounded crazy even to me. Susi left plenty of space in our conversation in case I wanted to speak my mind, but I asked questions about jazz and silk stockings instead.

She cranked up a Victrola while we washed the pots. Piano ragtime filled her room. It sounded like rain falling on tin cans. Susi took my hand and showed me a few steps of the Charleston. It felt completely foreign to dance face to face and touching another person. I stepped on Susi's toes twice and our foreheads collided before I retreated to the cot along the wall. Susi laughed at me, but I didn't mind watching her dance by herself.

We passed three days together. In the mornings, I helped her sort letters in the post office downstairs. In the afternoons, we walked the beach or the forest along the edge of town to get blue mussels, Indian tea, or firewood. I loved the quiet of only two people in a house, and Susi wasn't worried about money or what people think. I could have drifted there like an otter in kelp and never thought about yesterday or tomorrow or anyone following after me.

On our fourth evening together, a storm came through. Susi stoked the fire and stuffed the cracks around the windowpanes with rags. Rain whooshed against the dark windows, and we could hear the creak of trunks bending in the wind and the snap of broken branches. We ate smoked halibut and canned pears, and afterward, Susi pulled a drum out from under her cot. It was not a little hand drum either. It was a floor drum almost as big as Grandpa's.

"Whose is that?" I asked.

"Mine," she said.

She pulled my crate up to one side and sat on her cot across from me.

"Women don't drum," I said, and then I hated the sound of Grandpa in my voice.

Susi smiled just enough to show dimples. "Women don't *say* they drum."

She took drumsticks out from under her pillow,

leaving one where I could reach it. She gave a few solid thumps to the middle of the drum. Then she picked up speed and beat steadily on the worn place along the rim.

She began to hum with her eyes shut. When she opened her mouth to let the song out, no words came, only the rise and fall of her voice. The power of her singing made my hair stand up. I could feel in it the freedom of living on her own and the wail of grief from losing her man far away in the war.

I leaned forward in my seat, closed my eyes, and rested my palms around the sides of the drum. I could feel Susi's loneliness, but it wasn't sad or even angry. There was strength in her voice and her drumming.

I swayed my head forward and back and tapped with my fingers. The music stacked up inside me. I opened my mouth, but it wouldn't come up. Just as sometimes the food wouldn't go down.

I picked up the drumstick and followed Susi's rhythm, beating close to the rim on my side of the drum. I felt Grandpa's stern gaze in my mind, and it stopped me. But I felt something else too. When I breathed in, my lungs felt larger.

Susi caught my eye and smiled with more joy than I had ever seen in her. She didn't have to say it. This is what Indians do—all of us. It doesn't matter if we are cowboys or farmers or ironworkers or fishermen. We all drum. I picked up my drumstick again and followed Susi. The drumbeats grew harder, softer, faster, and then finally slower and deeper, moving to the middle of the drum. When we finished, we were sweating as if we'd run in the mountains.

The next morning, I swept the lobby and dusted the counter of the post office, and Susi worked on the ledger while we waited for the mail to come up the beach at low tide. A stranger rode along on the mail truck.

"Is it the tenth of October?" I asked Susi.

She nodded. "So this must be the museum man who wrote to Grandpa back in August."

"Mr. Glen," he announced, hopping off the truck. "From the Art Institute." He stretched out a bony hand, connected to an even scrawnier arm, connected to a coat hanger holding up his jacket. I looked at Susi, and Susi looked at me, but she was older, so she had to shake the skeleton.

"Someone has to take him to Grandpa's house," Susi said while he was out at the mail wagon bringing in his suitcase. "You've got the canoe."

I nodded, but something about that man made my skin crawl. Still, I'd promised Grandpa I would help.

"May I offer you a ride, sir?"

"Excellent," Mr. Glen said. "My luggage will arrive presently."

It turned out "presently" meant right before dark. We spent the day waiting for the museum man's luggage and hearing whole books full of what Mr. Glen called anthropology and we called neighbors. He had been with the Klamath and the Tillamook and half a dozen other tribes up the coast in Oregon and Washington. He had an opinion on each of them and their art. He went on at great length about how discriminating the Art Institute was and how they would pay handsomely for the right piece of carving.

When the truck finally came with Mr. Glen's luggage, Susi had to move all the postal files and her chair upstairs to make room in her little office for Mr. Glen's boxes and shipping crates. He insisted on putting them in a room with a lock.

After dinner, he said, "I am accustomed to the rough life. Set up a cot for me anywhere." As if we were the sort of people to have extra cots lying around not in use. Susi rolled out her blankets on the floor and hauled the cot downstairs.

"He's used to the rough life," I whispered to Susi. "Let's make him sleep out on the front porch."

Susi laughed it off. "Mr. Sharp-Sides would scratch

a hole in my good floors if I let him sleep on them," she said.

I could sleep on anything if I made up my mind to, but something old Sharp-Sides said during dinner stung my brain awake.

"Carver?" he said after we were fully introduced. "Are you the Carver family who keeps the whole cycle of Raven dances?"

"Yes," I said, and I might have said more, but I saw greed jump up like a flame in his eyes. Suddenly, he seemed to have eight tentacles on each hand, long and grasping like the devilfish.

I remembered what Grandpa said: "This man is looking to take from us."

No matter how hard I tried to sleep, I could see his greedy eyes looking at the chest of my father's dance masks. In my dreams, I saw coins dripping out of slippery, wet fingers that closed around the chest and dragged it to the bottom of the ocean.

The more I saw those long hands, the more I burned inside. I made a plan. I didn't wait for daylight.

# 11

## *The Seal Hunter's Beach*

I woke early the next morning, before the sun rose. I tiptoed around Susi's room by candlelight and gathered up my things. I left a note.

> *I am going to bring a bigger canoe and get Henry to help us bring Mr. Glen's luggage to Grandpa's house. If the weather gets bad, I'll stay at La Push.*

It was not exactly a lie, I told myself. Henry knew Mr. Glen was arriving, and he would come to get him eventually. I made a quick drawing for Susi: the forest, the mountains, the lake, and the colors, green, purple, and blue. I packed my things in the fish canoe and paddled away silently, as soon as it was light enough to see.

The air was dead calm, and thick fog hovered a few feet above the ocean. I should not have been out on the water that day. I should have faced the museum man and told him my father's things were not for sale, not at any price.

I paddled as quickly as I dared. Headlands and sea stacks were invisible to me. I navigated by counting freshwater inlets. The rain the night before last washed mud into all the rivers and creeks. Each stream spread a slim brown fan over the salt water. The lighthouse at Destruction Island was nothing but a color change in the clouds, and the Hoh River, swollen with rain, pushed at my paddle as I crossed its outflow.

After an hour on the water, the fog rose just enough to see the beach. La Push came next. I headed farther out to sea. The people of the village might recognize me from the shore. They might busybody themselves up the coast to Grandpa's house in Ozette and tell him I was coming before I had a chance to steal what was mine. I dipped my paddle quietly and pulled hard until I was past the Quileute Reservation.

Once I crossed the outlet of the Calawah River, I knew I was safe. Only empty beaches between there and Ozette. The relief of it made me giddy. I imagined men chasing me down the beach dressed like the Keystone Kops who were always chasing Charlie Chaplin. I snorted out a suppressed laugh. The honk of it made me giggle, and the giggling almost made me pee. The monstrous disrespect of peeing in my grandmother's fish canoe while planning cold-blooded theft of ceremonial objects and leaving my family forever made me laugh so hard, I had to set down my paddle. I held my sides in and clamped my knees together. Tears collected on the point of my chin and dripped into the collar of my coat. The echo of my laugh barked back at me.

A jolt of panic hit. There shouldn't be an echo over open water.

I swung my head around, peering through the shifting mist. There was barely time to see the shadow of an offshore rock before I lurched forward and struck my head on the gunwale. For a second, there was only the ring of the strike and the burst of white fireworks under my eyelids. When I sat up, black barnacle-speckled rocks towered over me. A split opened a little bit back from the bow. Cold seawater seeped into my canoe, and warm blood flowed down my face.

I seized my paddle and pushed against the rock. My canoe dragged a few inches lower, breaking off barnacles as it went. The split lengthened, and water gurgled in.

I scooted back in the boat to lift the bow. On the next wave, I shoved with my paddle again. A notch broke off the tip of it, but I was afloat.

I back-paddled with all my strength, looking over my shoulder, winking blood out of my eye. Another roll and the side of my canoe struck a smaller rock. I saw that one coming and braced myself, and the canoe held. The water was ankle-deep and rising. I fought my boat backward out of the cluster of offshore rocks. By the time I made open water, my arms were shaking with fatigue, and the boat was almost half full. I grabbed the bailer and flung water out. The beach seemed a million miles away. My hands were cramped with cold, and the darkness of the deep water all around froze my heart. I'd never make it. Even if I could swim, I'd freeze before I made the shore. My shoulders slumped, and I gave in to shivering.

A torpedo shape passed under my canoe. A sleek, dark head broke the surface one body length away. The seal stared at me with sorrowful brown eyes. A blink and he was gone, but he rose again on my other side and stared. The memory of my father's voice came to me.

"The whale will rise and rise again to offer his life."

Life.

He was offering me life.

I let the word throb in my head. Life.

I took up my paddle and sat tall like a whaler. The

wind was against me, but the tide was in my favor. I clamped my chattering teeth shut and dug in. The seal ducked down, showed his tail, and disappeared. All the extra water made my boat heavy. I gained the beach by inches. I was drenched. The muscles of my arms and back burned. Finally, I could see the sand under the breakers. I rolled out into chest-deep water and walked my boat in. I was so exhausted when my feet hit level sand, I collapsed in a heap with the dead kelp.

The October breeze got me on my feet. I tipped the water out of my canoe and searched for the tide line. A weathered beach log stuck out of the sand above the high-tide mark—the start of my shelter. I took the basket and food box out of the boat and stashed them by the log. My wet clothes sucked strength out of my body. I lifted the lid of the clothes basket. My things inside were dry.

"God bless Aunt Loula and her watertight basket," I whispered, and kicked off my wet things.

The shabby, hand-me-down wool blouse and skirt never looked so good. I rubbed as much of the water as I could off my bare skin and then shivered into the dry clothes.

The blankets were wet at both ends but dry in the middle because Grandpa had rolled them in an old cedar rain cape. I threw the cape over my shoulders and pulled on the fur mitts Henry had given me. When I sat with my knees hugged to my chest, the cape made a warming tent that reached the sand. I shivered and rubbed my arms and legs to bring up the heat of my blood.

When my hands were warm enough to move freely and my shivering slowed enough for a steady hand, I reached for the cut on the crown of my head. The wound was two fingers long, starting at the edge of my hairline above my left eye. The cut was spread open and bleeding, but not as fast as before. I probed it gently, feeling for splinters. There was nothing in the wound but the pillow of swelling underneath and the throb with each blood beat.

I closed my eyes to concentrate and squeezed the edges of the cut together.

"Skin wants to bond," Grandma always said when she was tending a knife wound. "It just takes patience."

I remembered once when Papa cut his hand carving, she held the edges of the cut together for an entire day. Then she bound his hand to the opposite shoulder for a week, so he would not break the new skin.

I forced my muscles to relax as I waited for the bleeding to stop. I leaned back against the log and took in the sky. The fog was clearing, but heavy clouds were coming in. It was going to rain. Probably after dark, when the tide was low. I thought over my needs. A fire was what I wanted, for noise and warmth and company, but shelter was what I needed, and time to make it. I couldn't measure how long it was until sunset with the cloud cover. Judging by hunger, it was late afternoon.

I released the cut on my head. The sides of the wound sprang apart and bled again. I kicked at the sand, fighting the urge to cry. I did not have time to wait. I squeezed the cut together again and brushed my hair over my shoulder. Even moving my hair made my scalp sting, but it gave me an idea. I carefully separated three small strands of hair around the cut and made a thin braid that pulled together the sides of the wound. The stickiness of the blood held my hair in place. It wasn't perfect. The end of the cut that went below my hairline was still open, but it stopped the bleeding. I took a deep breath and allowed myself a few tears of relief. Then I rubbed blood out of my hands with sand and thought about a shelter.

I checked the headlands at either end of the beach. Sometimes there was a cave or an overhanging rock above the tide line. No such luck, nothing but bare cliffs with a crown of stunted shore pines on top and a yellow-green dusting of lichen on the vertical sides. I tugged the canoe up the sand to the driftwood, flipped it upside down, and propped one end on the log. I mounded up sand around the bottom and stuck the basket and wet clothes underneath. The food box had a lid and would be fine left out in the rain.

It was beginning to get dark, and I was longing for the comfort of a campfire. What I really needed was cedar branches to keep dry. I dug the long knife out of the food box and searched the tree line for the profile of a cedar. Stubby shore pines edged the sand and alders clustered around a stream. Behind them I saw what I needed—tree of life. Western red cedar, the loggers called it.

I walked up the streambed, looking for a game trail to get through the underbrush. I didn't dare go deep into the rain forest. Even without the Pitch Woman and the Timber Giant, I might not find my way out. A close look at the stream bank showed pairs of moon prints from a mule deer. I searched the ferns and salal clustered on the ground for a game trail. It was less than a hand's width wide and curved inland away from the stream. I stopped to listen for bears and wolves. I searched up in the tree branches for a cougar. I whispered a quick prayer and stepped into the woods.

Plenty of fresh cedar branches littered the ground from the storm two nights ago. I hacked them into a manageable size with the long knife and dragged as many as I could behind me.

I was back at the creek before I remembered the song to thank the cedars. The one that I knew was a baby song. My mother sang a different one, a more dignified song for women. I hadn't been old enough to learn it when she died. I could only sing the one I knew. I did my best, but the forest swallowed up my song. I ran for the beach and did not look back.

It began to rain. I draped the cedar branches over the canoe. They reached down to the sand and the water rolled off them the way a bird's feathers shed rain. I climbed under my shelter, rolled up in blankets, and fell asleep listening to the waves.

Hunger woke me, or maybe cold. I lifted my head and groaned. Maybe it was my aching body that woke me. It was hard to settle on a chief misery that morning. I stuck my head and shoulders out of the shelter and grabbed smoked salmon and berry cake from the food box. I propped myself up on my elbows and devoured breakfast.

The cut on my head had a rock-solid scab with no oozing infection underneath. It was the only fragment of good news I could think of. A ribbon of light showed through the split on the bow of my canoe. I put on the rain cape and rolled out from underneath. From the outside, I could see it was an impact split. All the wood was still there. It was fixable. The notch broken off of my paddle was a lost cause. I could still use it, but I'd have to work harder for each stroke.

It was still raining. Fog too. There was no sound of passing boats, and I wondered for a moment what would happen when Susi realized I had not gone to get a bigger canoe to bring Mr. Glen and his luggage to Grandpa's house. The fog worked in my favor there. No one would try to travel in this weather. I might still have time to save my father's dance masks, if I could make a patch for my boat out of pitch and pine needles. I turned away from the ocean. Pine sap, a fire, and a sheltered place to work had my attention for the rest of the day.

There was a cluster of tall rocks beside the cliff at the north end of the beach. They would protect me from the wind. There was an hour before high tide. I took the knife and scored the trunks of a dozen shore pines to make the sap run free. When the tide was all the way up, I put my gear in the boat, dragged it to the water, and floated it to the north end of the beach. The rocks made my campsite feel more sheltered. I collected scraps of driftwood for my fire and dug around trees for dry needles. I made a proper fire ring with rocks, determined not to pass another night without the company of flames. There was a break in the rain, so I draped the blankets on the shorter rocks to dry in the wind and headed back into the trees.

Collecting sap was a miserable job. No wonder Grandpa always made Charlie do it. I scraped and scratched and rolled for hours to get a wad of pitch half the size of a baseball. It was probably not enough. I cut a dozen more strips out of the bark, in case I needed more tomorrow.

I passed a rosebush on my way back to the beach and picked a pocketful of rose hips for tea. There were brake ferns nearby, so I pulled up roots to roast for supper. Back on the beach, I built a fire. It took an hour to get it from flicker to heat. By the time the pitch was hot enough to work, it was nearly too dark to see. Before I quit for the night, I put the remains of the pitch up on a rock to keep the sand off. I set the roots on to roast and dropped a hot rock in a bowl for tea. A minute later, a downpour drowned my fire.

"It is only rain," I told myself. "God does not hate me." I rolled up in a ball under my canoe and shivered my blankets warm. Bad dreams followed me into the dark. I heard my name called and I followed, but each calling led me to a stone that blocked my path.

# 12

# *The Discovery*

The next morning broke bright and clear. As soon as the sun was a handsbreadth over the mountains, steam rose all around me. I climbed one of the beach rocks to look over the water for passing boats. I had to scramble to find handholds. I pulled myself up slowly, resting my chest on the top while I swung a leg up over the edge of the stone.

As I got to my feet, I saw a tiny pool of water by my hand. It was perfectly round, with a little island in the middle like the letter *O*. I straightened up, shaded my eyes, and looked over the breakers to the cluster of rocks where my boat had run aground a day and a half ago.

Three seals lounged in the sun, the waves licking their back flippers.

Which one raised his head to me? I wondered. Which

one sent me here to the seal hunter's beach? I smiled and almost waved at them. The wind pushed the rising mist off the sand and into the trees. All my plans seemed possible under this cold blue sky.

I looked down at the rock and gasped. Sunlight reflecting on a dozen shallow pools of water shined like a shield of copper. Smoothly curved narrow channels of water, ovoids large and little, made a hammered jewel on flat rock.

I knelt and dipped my fingers in. The edges of the pool were smooth, with crumbs in the bottom left over from grinding. I imagined a hand. A stone. A million strikes of the mallet—all done in some unseen past.

I walked slowly around the edge of the shining pools of water. When my body faced north, I saw him: Chitwin, the face of the Bear with eyes, teeth, a square head, and small ears. The sight of him made every hair on my body stand up. It was the same face that looked out half-finished from Mama's loom. The same face I had seen somewhere else long ago, glowing. I probed that memory, and after a few moments, it unfolded. Mama's button blanket looked like this, with the face of Chitwin outlined in pearl buttons.

I spread my arms, imagining the weight of a robe of power over my shoulders. I took a step to the north, slow and heavy, and then another. The face of Bear was my fire. I stepped quicker, lighter, turning my shoulders to face the fire and then the sky, as Mama had done. I remembered her dance and the story that each step told.

I danced the whole story of Bear walking out of the mountains in spring to bring the summer berries. When I finished, arms out and face up to the sun, I felt light pour into my body. I squeezed my eyes shut, my hands in fists to keep that filled-up feeling in.

"This is mine," I announced to rocks and air. "Mine forever. No pencil-pointy, paper-thin stranger will take it from me."

I danced the story through again, singing the Bear chant this time to fix it in my mind. I stroked my finger around the outline of Bear's face one last time and jumped down to the sand.

Three more beach rocks stood in a cluster by my camp. Two were jagged on top, with white streaks from nesting birds. I circled them, but they were just rocks with no climb holds. The third was as tall as Grandpa's house and flat-topped with a smooth landward face. At shoulder height, I saw a cluster of carved spirals, shallow and weathered at the edges. The south edge of the rock had a few outcroppings and a seam that ran nearly straight to the top.

I tucked my skirt into my waistband and set one bare foot against the stone. I wedged my fingers into the seam and pulled myself up. I hunted with my toes for the next foothold, settled my balance, and wiped a sweaty hand on the back of my blouse. Fingers inched along the crevice, and I shifted my weight to the upper leg to hunt for another foothold.

I laughed out loud, loving the stretch and pull on my muscles, the wind flapping my clothes, the victory of leaving the ground. By the time I hauled myself over the top, I had white scratch marks on my knees and rock crumbs in my hair.

I could see at once that I'd found a treasure. This rock carving was larger, sharper, maybe newer? I stepped carefully around the edge looking for right side up. This carving faced west.

There was a whale, openmouthed with an upturned tail. Blue-green flakes of weathered copper were pounded into the skin to make it shimmer. Two canoes were underneath the whale, with three peaked hats in each to show whalers. On the landward side of the picture was a human face with its eyes closed and mouth open. Singing? Praying? I wished I knew.

I studied the carving from all sides, drinking in the details, searching out the meaning of the maker. A whaler's prayer, I decided. His hope. His need to feed his family. His legacy for his sons and grandsons.

Did my father carve this stone? Did he leave it for

his family, to say this is who I am, a whaler? I scanned the stone for some mark of the maker, a symbol, a signature style. I saw nothing familiar, but stone is not as easy to work as cedar. Still, some whaler made this. Spent his hours and months in the company of shorebirds and stone to say this to the sky forever.

"Why didn't anybody tell me about this before?" I said aloud. It was odd. Why should this carving be a secret hidden from all who passed by but didn't know where to look? Every other carving my family made—totem, mask, canoe—was a public work meant to proclaim the strength and prosperity of our name. Why would this stone carving be kept a secret from all but passing birds? I thought about what had brought me there. Why was my first impulse, when Papa's masks were in danger, to steal them, hide them, and run away? Away to some white town—not Aberdeen, where people might know my family, but Seattle or Victoria or Vancouver. Someplace where my face would be nothing but another immigrant in the dozens that walked off every train and boat.

I imagined that life. Me, alone in the city, working as a washerwoman or living in one of those orphanages where they taught you to be a white person. How to stand and dress and pray, until the bread-loaf brown faded from my skin and the words of my childhood were erased like chalk marks. What a grub they would make of me, a pale, blind weevil that thinks of filling its belly and nothing more. I raised a fist against that path. Something worse than the Pitch Woman would be waiting for me at the end of that road.

I paced the edge of the whaler's rock carving. It was the whale I loved first, with his ocean-green copper skin. The arch of his body stretched over the entire seaward side of the stone. I did not like the canoes as much. Something was wrong with them, a mistake. Their prows faced away from the whale. They did not lie side by side as boats in the ocean did to meet the current and wind straight on. They made a downward-pointing V.

Unless.

I walked around to the whale side of the carving. Unless the canoes were an arrow, an arrow that pointed to—the teller.

I felt a rush of warmth in my hands and a drumbeat in my heart. This was the meaning of the openmouthed man. He was the teller, the one who went from family to family and even to other villages to tell the story. It was the teller who made whaling true. What happened at sea was a mystery. Only the ones who went on the hunt knew, but one whaler came home to tell and made every moment of the hunt real to all Makah who listened.

Papa was that teller. I could be the teller now. I could make his life real. I could raise him out of the water with words. The thought sang through my whole body. Pearl Carver, daughter of whalers, tell this story.

I scampered down the side of the stone, threw open my basket, and pulled out my diary. I flipped past the first three pages—the names of my family—and smoothed open a fresh page.

Words rushed out of my pencil, the name of this place, the time of year, the position of the carved stones. Then I sketched each carving and wrote the names of Bear and Whale.

On the Bear page, I wrote Mama's song and the steps of her dance. I wrote the story her dance told, the design of her button blanket.

I paused for a moment at the Whale page. A whaler guarded his knowledge, passing it only to grown sons. There were three men left in Grandpa's family: Uncle Jeremiah, Henry, and Charlie. What if they went away to lumber camps or mining camps or army camps and never came home. I thought of the storyteller on the rock. I must not shut that open mouth. Who but me would do this?

I scooped a more comfortable sitting spot in the sand and leaned against the warm side of the stone. I wrote small and filled the pages edge to edge, barely keeping up with the words that surged from my throat in whispers, songs, and shouts. I put in accent marks for clarity, and invented letters for Quinault and Makah sounds that didn't exist in English. I left blank spaces for things I would need to ask Grandma about, facts and names I should double-check. My fingers tingled as I wrote the way they did high in the mountains. When I got stuck for a word, I drew footprints across the top of the page. My children's footprints, my grandchildren, they were leading me now.

I wrote for hours, until my pencil was an inch shorter and half the pages of my diary were full. I ate my food cold that night and didn't bother with a fire. The stars and my words on the page were company enough. I put aside all thoughts of mending the boat and decided to spend at least a week walking the beach and looking for more stone carvings to record.

That night, I dreamed of a boat. I was in a long canoe. It was as finely made as a whaling canoe, but it was no boat I had been in before. A tall cream-colored sail swelled with a steady wind and carried me west, the direction from which all good things come. The sail was covered top to bottom with words in my own handwriting.

The next morning, I checked my reserve of food. There were two meals left in my box, three if I stretched them, but I could gather beach food from the tide pools if I got hungry. Sea urchin was not my favorite, but it was easy to find and fix.

I decided to visit the Chitwin carving after eating. I scrambled to the top of the shorter beach rock. The morning was overcast but not foggy, and the lines of the Bear's face were not quite as spectacular as they had been in full sun the day before. I loved them anyway.

I searched again for a signature mark. Every artist did something. It might be the shape of the eye in a totem pole or a certain color always placed around the lid of a basket. Mama signed her weaving with a yellow-and-black nine-square checkerboard, very small in the right-hand corner. I saw nothing that resembled a maker's mark, but maybe after I had found more of these stone pictures I would be able to read them better.

Barking sounds from the ocean caught my ear, and I glanced out to the seal rocks. Two larger seals were fighting over a resting spot, or maybe they were fighting over the smaller female who watched them struggle with avid interest. In the middle of their shoving match, the female lifted her head, looked north, and gave a short bark. In the blink of an eye, all three dove and disappeared. By instinct, I did the same, jumping down from my watching place and hiding behind the beach rock to see what came from the north.

It was Uncle Jeremiah's canoe, the big one with the Raven carving on the prow. It was close enough to shore that I could hear Henry and Uncle Jeremiah's muffled voices. Were they looking for me, or were they going to bring Mr. Glen to Grandpa's house? I could have gone down to the water and called to them. They would have given me a ride. But I hated the idea of being rescued. The thought of explaining my reckless voyage and towing my broken boat home was too much to take. I weighed my pride. There was still time to fix the canoe and make it home before them, time to decide what to do about my father's regalia. The notion of stealing it and running away seemed a hollow and foolish choice now. Something Ida would do, not me.

I set my diary aside, promising myself it would only be for a day. A half hour of scrounging firewood and another hour of collecting pine pitch had me ready to work. It was a dull and messy business to warm the pitch on the end of a stick and then work it into the crack in the bow of my canoe. I filled the split and reinforced it with pine needles, working both from the inside and outside of the boat. Once the sap cooled and hardened, I tested the bond by pouring water over it, and then by dragging the canoe to the surf and holding the bow down in the water. It wasn't a tidy-looking repair, but it held.

I decided to skip lunch to get home before dark. Even so, the sun was only one fist up from the horizon and a soft rain was falling when I pulled onto the beach in front of the village. The sand was empty and doors were closed, but yellow lamplight spilled out of windows, and the smell of wood smoke, biscuits, and elk stew was welcome enough.

I opened the door of Grandpa's house to find the floor freshly swept and a table set for nine. Grandma was rolling biscuits for a second batch. Ida was hustling food to the table, and Charlie was filling the wood box. Aunt Loula flapped up to me with an apron in one hand and a soup ladle in the other.

"Back already?" she said. "Where are the men?"

"We came in two boats and mine is much lighter. I'm sure they're only a little ways behind me." I smiled, followed her to the kitchen, and started ladling soup into a long wooden dish. She believed me. What a relief. I would eventually have to answer for running off, but with a little luck it wouldn't be tonight.

Ida scampered back and forth between the table and the front door, and about a half hour later, she let out a squeak and began to jump and spin, shouting, "They're home! They're home!"

Aunt Loula snatched off her apron and Ida's, washed her hands, and smoothed her hair. Grandpa wrapped a button blanket around his shoulders, and Grandma looked pointedly at my sweaty blouse and stained skirt.

I ducked into my room and snatched the only clean dress off the pegs on the wall. I could hear Uncle Jeremiah and Henry and Mr. Glen come in the door. Grandpa met them with formal style and made the introductions, quoting ancestors back five generations. I skidded into place behind Charlie just as Grandpa came to my lineage. He said the names of my mother's parents and grandparents and the name of their village with as much pride as his own family line.

I looked Mr. Glen in the face and shook his hand the way the schoolmaster taught us to do. I gave him a hard look and was surprised to see how small he seemed in my own house standing next to my uncle and grandfather. His thin body was as curved as a question mark, and I heard nothing of the pompous tone he had taken in a house of just women.

He made a brief thank-you speech after Grandpa finished his welcome, and I heard nothing of the greed that had spooked me back at the post office. Still, I did not trust him. He spoke kindly, even generously, but I looked for a lie in his words.

All through dinner, Mr. Glen plied Grandpa with questions about our reservation. Grandpa kept telling about the ocean and the strength of the fish runs, and Mr. Glen kept asking about the land.

Charlie thought it was hilarious, although he knew enough to hide it while he was at the table. He kept score with peas on his plate of how many land questions Mr.

Glen asked and how many ocean answers Grandpa gave. I didn't hear the lie I was listening for. Did I hate Mr. Glen for being a white man, the way the lady in town hated me for being an Indian?

When dinner was finished and Grandpa led the guest to his room, Henry leaned toward me and whispered, "How did you manage to paddle past La Push without being seen by a soul? Susi said you would be there, but they didn't know anything about it."

I checked to see if he was angry, but he smiled as though he had caught me doing something secretly clever.

"Magic," I said.

Henry laughed, and Grandma looked at me from across the table as if to say, just because I'm not asking doesn't mean I don't know you've been up to something.

# 13

## *Home Again*

That night, as I listened to the welcome sigh of Ida sleeping in the bunk above me, I thought about how I would fill the rest of my diary. There must be more of the stone carvings. I would find an excuse to walk the beaches near the village to look for them. There were caves and beaches north of us that no one used. But the cold rains were coming, and I would be shut up at home for days at a time over the winter. I decided to spend that time getting Grandma to tell me things I wanted to learn about the Bear stories and the regalia my mother wore.

In the morning, after breakfast, Mr. Glen dressed in a jacket and cap and waited by the door as if he was expecting the grand tour of local curiosities. Grandpa had other plans. His carving bench was set out with the mask he was working on that week. Henry sat at the other end of the bench stirring fish oil into his paints to freshen them.

"That man," tutted Grandma over the dishes. "Where did he learn his manners?"

Grandpa took up his work, plainly annoyed that Mr. Glen was ignoring him. Uncle Jeremiah and Aunt Loula talked quietly at the far end of the room. I figured they were making plans about how to best part Mr. Glen from some of his money. Charlie surfaced from devouring his third helping of oatmeal and grabbed his coat.

"Really, Mr. Glen," he said. "You don't have to help me get the firewood. I can manage alone. Come sit by the workbench. It's warm, and I'm sure Grandpa has valuable stories to tell you."

It worked. Mr. Glen headed reluctantly to the middle of the room. No wonder Charlie was Grandpa's favorite.

"May I make you some tea?" I said.

"Tea would be very nice," Mr. Glen answered. He sat and took a small notebook out of his pocket. It gave me an idea.

As soon as I'd fixed the tea, I got my diary and pencil from my room. I shaved a sharper point with the folding knife and settled on a bench near Henry, where I could hear what Grandpa said without being noticed. I set a bundle of sweetgrass beside me on the bench so I'd look busy, and wound the first few coils of a basket.

Grandpa worked with the short knife, forming a mouth and teeth on the Wolf mask. He explained with care how he harvested fresh wind-fallen cedars and let the logs dry for many months before working them.

I started a new page in my diary and tried to keep up with Grandpa's voice. I left blank spaces where I wanted to ask a question. I managed to fill four pages edge to edge, but Mr. Glen didn't appear to be listening.

"He's not very curious, is he?" Henry said quietly. He leaned closer so he could see my page. "He's certainly not as curious as you."

I flipped the book shut and slid it under the pile of sweetgrass. There was probably a rule about who was allowed to write, and if it wasn't women's work, I didn't want to hear about it.

Henry glanced at Mr. Glen to be sure he was ignoring us, then said, "A businessman in town keeps a record of everything that happens in his shop. It makes it hard to steal from him." He nodded in the direction of my book. "We should do the same. It's good business."

"I don't trust him," I said.

Henry smiled. "Susi mentioned that when we were down getting Mr. Glen and his luggage. She said he wanted to buy your father's Raven regalia."

"I don't want to sell it," I whispered, forcing my voice to be soft and my expression calm. I glanced at Grandpa and the visitor again. "I don't care. I'll go get a cannery job to make up the money if that's what's important." I wanted to go on and tell him how those masks and dance robe belonged to my sons and grandsons and nobody else had a right to them, but I was pretty sure I would cry if I did.

Henry thought for a moment and said, "I don't trust him either. In fact, I'm not sure he is an art collector at all. On the ride up here, I asked him about Boas and Eammons and a few of the other famous art collectors from a dozen years ago. He didn't seem to know any of them."

"What's he doing here, then?" I whispered back.

"We'll have to follow him to find out," Henry said. "I have an idea about how to learn if he's an art collector and keep him away from your dad's Raven masks at the same time. Want to help?"

I nodded.

"I need to talk to Mr. Glen in private. If you see me leave the house with him, find an excuse to tag along."

I nodded again, and we both went back to looking busy with basket weaving and repainting the carved lid of an old cedar chest.

We didn't have a chance to test Henry's idea until the next day. It was still raining, not a storm but a steady cold rain that hinted at winter storms to come. Uncle Jeremiah and Aunt Loula had done their best all morning to interest Mr. Glen in basket making and the process for steam-bending cedar boards to make a chest.

Henry came in from hauling water and said, "It's clearing up. Would you enjoy a walk?"

Mr. Glen jumped at the offer like a dog that hadn't seen a bone in a week.

"You're almost out of maidenhair ferns for the baskets," I said to Aunt Loula. "I'll go pick some more."

"And hemlock bark," Grandma said, looking up from her basketwork. "We don't have near enough with cold and cough season coming on."

"I'll bring back plenty of both," I said, skipping toward the door.

Henry took us only a dozen yards or so from the house to an open woodshed that stood at the edge of the rain forest. It had four pillars, a roof, and one wall.

"Is this a whaler's bathhouse?" Mr. Glen asked eagerly.

"Obviously not," Henry said, looking pointedly at me. Henry would never take someone, not even Charlie, to such a secret place. I wondered how a man smart enough to work at a museum could mistake a shed full of half-worked wood for anything else. Henry went to the back of the shed and picked up a bundle wrapped in oilcloth.

"I understand you are interested in buying the Raven regalia belonging to my uncle, Victor Carver," he said.

My heart lurched. He wouldn't.

"Yes," Mr. Glen said. "A colleague described it. Many years ago, he saw the Raven stories danced up in Alaska. It was, how did he call it, a transformation mask."

"We must be secret about this," Henry said, stepping closer to the man. "My parents and grandparents are very traditional."

"Yes," Mr. Glen said even more eagerly. "I noticed that."

"Here it is," Henry said with a flourish, and he unveiled his own Owl mask.

I gasped, and Mr. Glen took the hint and gasped as well. What was Henry thinking? He would never pull it off. A child of three could tell you an owl has a curved beak and a raven a straight one.

"Does it transform into a man?" Mr. Glen asked in an awed whisper.

"Of course." Henry turned the mask so we could see the inside. "This is the string and toggle that go under the cedar neck ring and down the dancer's sleeve."

"And when you pull the string?" he asked.

Henry pulled the string and the mask opened like a mouth, showing another mask underneath. "The face of a man."

"Beautiful," Mr. Glen breathed. "Do you have any idea what this is worth to the right buyer?"

I shook my head in disbelief. How could anyone not know that the Moon goes with the Owl story? The inner mask was too round to be a man's face, and it was painted white.

"Name your price," Mr. Glen said.

"What will your buyer pay?" Henry asked.

Mr. Glen paused to calculate. "There was a second mask," he said, "and a cape of black feathers."

My heart skipped a beat. Henry had nothing he could pass off as the Raven cape. There was no other regalia even close.

"A feather cape doesn't last," Henry lied. "Vermin get into it, and fleas. After a few years it falls apart."

Mr. Glen nodded as if he were receiving bad news from a doctor. "But the second mask, the Raven's head that transforms into the Sun?"

I knew the one Mr. Glen meant. It was the most intricate mask my family owned. It split along four lines to make eight points of the Sun's rays. Each point was lined with burnished copper that caught the firelight when my father danced. It burst open at the part of the story where Raven released the Sun.

"It's damaged," I blurted out. "Burned. It wouldn't be worth anything now."

Mr. Glen glared at me.

"I'm sorry," I mumbled. "It's true."

"It was old," Henry chimed in as smoothly as if we had planned this. "I can make you another. Its twin exactly. Advance me fifty dollars for copper plate and you can have it in a few weeks' time."

"It will be the one my buyer remembers?" he asked.

Henry promised, and Mr. Glen heaved a sigh of relief. "That's very good news."

"Come," Henry said warmly. "You've been cooped up inside for two days, and I can tell you're eager to see our land. Let's walk."

We took a short trail to the beach and turned north. We hadn't gone half a mile when Mr. Glen took out pocket binoculars and studied the shore for several minutes. Another half mile, and he did the same. Henry and I stepped a few yards away from him to talk.

Henry leaned toward me and whispered, "He can't possibly be what he claims to be. He doesn't speak a word of our language or any other worth knowing. He has heard about your father's Raven dances from somebody, but he's plainly never heard our stories. I remember those other museum men who came when I was little. They knew about us, and they were very competitive with each other."

"Look at him, though." I tilted my head in the museum man's direction. "He's looking for something. Do you think he's a grave robber?"

It made my skin crawl to think of it. There used to be museums that would pay ten dollars for an Indian skull, twenty dollars if all the bones came with it.

"We have to find a way to let him look for what he wants without letting him keep what he finds," Henry said.

"He thinks he's smarter than we are," I said. "Maybe we can make that work for us."

Henry smiled. "Let him think we're trusting and defenseless. We'll show him in the end."

Trusting, I thought. I put that personality on like a costume. I slumped my shoulders and walked up to Mr. Glen with a gait more like Ida than Aunt Susi. I looked him straight in the face.

"Beautiful, isn't it." I gestured to the sweep of silver-green forest combing the low clouds that came off the water.

"Mmm." He nodded. "It's so pristine and empty."

I struggled to keep a blank face. I had never in my life thought of our land as empty. The Quileute lived a few miles south of us, and the entire Makah nation bordered us to the north. On our short walk, I'd already seen elk and bear tracks and the face of a raccoon in the trees. I had heard tree frogs and a dozen kinds of birds.

"I've traveled to more than thirty of our forty-eight

states, and I must say, Miss Pearl, this is the most lush and rugged landscape I have seen."

"What did you do in all those other places?"

Mr. Glen hesitated a moment and looked over his shoulder to see that Henry was several steps behind. "I must confess," he said quietly. "I am something of an artist myself."

That was the whopper of all lies. Mr. Glen had the artistic sense of a banana slug. Something had to be behind that claim.

"I thought you might be," I said with an encouraging smile.

"Photography," he announced. "Landscape photography, mostly. I've amassed quite a collection in my travels, and I hope to make a name for myself." He shrugged and added, "I am a rock hunter as well, a minor hobby for my own personal collection."

"So you want to see our best landscapes and most interesting rocks while you're here?"

"Exactly." He smiled. "Discreetly, of course. My official mission is to collect cultural artifacts."

"I see," I said, stalling a little to form a plan. I drew him a few more steps ahead of Henry, who took the hint and dropped farther behind us.

"I could take you where you want to go in the

afternoon. Tell my grandfather . . ." I searched for a plausible lie and remembered the herb gathering Grandma had asked me to do.

"Tell him you are taking a survey of medicine plants. I know all of Grandma's herbs, and she would rather have me do it than walk around in the cold herself."

"An ethnobotany," Mr. Glen murmured. "Yes, that would work."

He turned to me and smiled a narrow, pointed smile. "You are a clever girl, Pearl. A photographer's assistant makes a half-dollar a day in the city. I propose to pay you for your services." He stuck out his hand.

I bit the inside of my cheek to keep from cringing and shook his bony fingers.

# 14

## *Above Shipwreck Cove*

If I had known that a photographer's assistant had to lug the camera gear around, I would have made Charlie do it. I spent the next three afternoons carrying a canvas knapsack full of gear up and down trails and beaches. Mr. Glen had a metal tripod to use with his camera and something that seemed to be a one-eyed binocular. Whenever Mr. Glen used it, he wrote columns of figures in a palm-sized notebook with a fountain pen. When he thought I was busy picking chanterelles or gathering herbs, he would unfold a map of the coast and make marks on it.

He did take pictures, plenty of them. He favored open sites for the natural light, and he paid particular attention to the lay of the land and any unusual rock formations.

He taught me to take pictures so he could be in some of them. But I didn't need to wait for the prints to see there was nothing artistic about his photographs.

On the fourth afternoon, Mr. Glen said, "We should have a look at the land above what you call Shipwreck Cove."

I was afraid he might ask to go there. There were many places nearby I was allowed to go, trails that led to camas meadows or berry fields, but the area above Shipwreck Cove was a burn site five generations back and off-limits to everyone. Even Grandpa didn't go there. The skeleton of a 150-year-old pirate ship marked the beach. No one ever explained how such a large ship had run aground there. The hints were dark.

I put him off with a lame excuse about being too tired to walk that far.

"Fine," he said. "If you don't want the four bits I'm paying you, I'll go on my own."

"It's dangerous up there," I said. As soon as the words were out, I regretted them.

"Your demon stories don't scare me," he said. "And I'm surprised that a girl your age who's been to school would give such silly superstitions a thought."

"Yes, sir." I ground my teeth and swallowed back a proud answer. Let him go. He could find out about evil all on his own. A few minutes later, when Mr. Glen had left the house, Henry hurried over with his spare shirt in hand.

"I've lost a button," he said loudly enough for Grandpa to hear over at his carving bench. "Let's take it outside where the light is better."

Once we got to the front porch, he whispered, "You let him get away alone! What's going on?"

"He wanted to go up above Shipwreck Cove," I whispered.

Henry swore under his breath. "That is the last place he should walk unwatched." He grabbed my hand and pulled me down the porch steps. "Come on," he said. "It's time you learned how to stalk prey." He took his spare brown work shirt and threw it over my shoulders to cover my light blue sweater and navy skirt.

"Follow me. Don't speak."

I went along behind him, noticing and copying the way he placed each foot with care, lifting so that there was no sound of a footfall or a rolling rock. In a few minutes, we were in earshot of Mr. Glen. It was like following a hippopotamus. He took no care to move quietly. He hummed a tune. He talked to himself.

There was a trail to the cove—a narrow one not often used, but it was definitely too wide for a game trail. We had to go a lot slower on that trail to keep from making noise when branches rubbed against our bodies.

When I was younger and I passed the trail to Shipwreck Cove, I wanted to sneak down and discover its secrets. Charlie and I made a game of guessing what sort of unnamed monster lived there and the vengeance he would take if we disturbed his home. But now, as I set out on the forbidden trail, even with the solid company of my oldest cousin, I felt dread grow.

We wound uphill around dead falls and outcroppings of rock. When we came to the top of the headland by Shipwreck Cove, the smell hit us. It was like rotting flesh, but more bitter. I drew back a few steps. Henry shook his head and motioned me forward. If the smell bothered him, he didn't show it. I could think of nothing but the stench. As we inched toward the treeless acres of burned stumps, meadow grass, and shoulder-high columns of mud in the saddle of land above the cove, the smell made my eyes water. Maybe I was smelling the rotting souls of the pirates that had died in that ship on the sand.

At the edge of the burn, Henry and I hid behind a cedar as broad as a barn door. The side of the tree that faced the ocean was blackened from its roots to fifty feet up, but the landward side was green and growing.

Down in the open area, Mr. Glen had put a red bandanna over his face train-robber-style to cut the foul odor. He approached a mud chimney, walked all the way around, measured it with a marked string, and took a picture. Then he held his hand over the top. Whatever he found in that chimney, it made him very happy.

Next, he moved to the rock wall at the north end of the meadow.

"An earthquake sometimes raises up a wall," Henry explained in a whisper. "And a mud chimney grows when there is fuel underground."

I nodded, remembering that Grandpa had showed me the layers of rock on a different wall years ago. He'd said each color stood for something.

Mr. Glen had apparently heard the same thing because he was digging a sample rock from each layer in the wall. He wrapped them in muslin and placed them in his sack, making notes on each one. Then he circled around closer to us, to the part of the meadow where the grass had gone yellow in a long oval patch.

Henry and I drew back behind the tree so he wouldn't see us, and turned our ears to listen. We heard Mr. Glen grunt and squat down. We heard the clack and thud of rocks being lifted and rolled out of the way.

"Eureka!" The museum man laughed aloud. He took something from his backpack, replaced it, and then walked out the way we came.

I was bursting with questions, but Henry held his

hand up to silence me until long after we could no longer hear Mr. Glen walking away.

"What is this place?" I asked. "What makes that smell?"

"Grandpa would call it a power of the earth," Henry said. "A power the museum man wants for himself."

"But he only took rocks," I said. I walked carefully up to the cone of mud to see what Mr. Glen was looking at. The stench was definitely coming from in there.

"This is the place where the power under the earth breathes," Henry said. He took a yellow-and-brown speckled maple leaf and held it over the mud chimney. The leaf fluttered up as if a gentle wind had caught it. A chill crawled up my back. I imagined some hideous creature breathing down in a stone chamber underground.

Henry walked slowly around the mud chimney, bent over to search the ground.

"And this is what he was looking for," Henry said.

He picked up a fist-sized black rock that was smooth and had a bit of luster to it, but it was not the mirror shine of black obsidian. Henry put the rock in his pocket and walked to the patch of yellowed grass.

The ground was steeply folded there. At the bottom of the crease was a black puddle. Henry dipped his finger in the puddle, and when he lifted his hand, the black liquid coated his finger. It was thicker than paint but not so stiff as glue. It smelled sharp and sour, but it didn't make my eyes water the way the mud chimney did.

"What could he possibly want this stuff for? It's ugly and smelly and—"

"And it burns," Henry said. "It's like whale oil but not so clean. I'll show you."

He scooped up a bit of the black oil with a shell and took me away from the burned area. Back in the trees, we found a moss-covered log. He set down the shell and the black stone and took a matchbox out of his pocket. When he touched a lit match to the oil in the shell, it burned with a blue flame, yellow at the edges, and gave off a thin black wisp of smoke. Then he took a knife and shaved a few crumbs off the black stone. He had to coax that one along, but after the third match it burned.

"Listen to me, Pearl," Henry said. "This coal and the oil and the natural gas that comes out of the chimney are all the same thing, and the gas catches fire most easily. You must never, never come here with fire."

"Is that why the ground is burned back in the clearing?"

Henry nodded. "When Grandpa's father was a boy, lightning struck one of those mud chimneys. There was an explosion they heard miles away and a pillar of fire taller than any tree."

"So it's not a monster?"

Henry smiled but not to mock me. "I don't believe in the old monsters, Pearl. Sometimes I wish I did. Is it worse to be swallowed by a demon or a fire?"

I thought it over and poked at the smoldering ashes with a twig.

"Monster," I decided. "With a monster, you always get a chance to trick your way back to life. At least you do in the good stories."

"We had better hang on to those good stories then." Henry took a wet piece of moss and dabbed out the last sparks. "When Grandma's gone there will only be you and me and Ida and Charlie to keep the old stories."

"Yes, and what if . . ." My mind jumped from sickness to war to logging accidents. "I'm going to write them down," I said firmly. "All of them."

"That's your father in you talking. He wasn't afraid to try new things." Henry laughed a little. "It drove my dad crazy, Grandpa too. But I admired that about him, and so did many other young men. When there was trouble in town or a dispute with a neighbor, Victor was the man people turned to."

"People always told me how brave he was," I said. "But I thought they were talking about whaling."

"Oh, he had the courage from the strength of his body," Henry said. "And so does many a fool who can't imagine his own death. But your father had courage from the strength of his ideas too, and that is what made him a leader of men."

The strength of his ideas, I thought. Now that's something of my father's I want to keep in my pocket.

"I wish he was here," Henry said. "I'd give a hundred coppers to know what he would have done about our museum man."

"What is Mr. Glen going to do?"

Henry shrugged. "He'll need investors in order to buy drilling equipment."

"They can't just drill. It's our land. We have a treaty to say so."

"Seems like a treaty doesn't count for much when you've got oil or gold or some other thing white people want on your reservation."

I nodded, looking at the ground. My friend Anita from Nitinat had cousins in Montana. They used to live in the Black Hills, but gold miners came and now they live in a rail-yard shack in Helena with strangers all around them and no clean water or view of the mountains. The schoolmaster called it assimilation. He called it admirable. I knew piracy when I saw it.

# 15

## *The Poker Game*

That night at dinner, Mr. Glen was more cheerful and talkative than he had been all week. He complimented Grandma and Aunt Loula extravagantly on their cooking and tried to make jokes with Uncle Jeremiah.

At the end of the meal he gestured for silence and announced, "Simon, Jeremiah, I have decided to buy the totem pole you are working on. It will be a fine addition to the Art Institute."

Aunt Loula gasped with pleasure, and Ida actually jumped up and clapped. I looked down at my hands and wished with all my heart for the Pitch Woman to swoop in the door and devour that man. There were smiles and handshakes all around. I noticed Henry making a charade of pleasant congratulations, so I did my best to disguise my feelings.

"A down payment of one hundred dollars. No, one hundred twenty," Mr. Glen went on. "And then another three hundred dollars when you deliver it in six months. How does that sound?"

Uncle Jeremiah smiled, and Grandpa nodded. Aunt Loula tapped her fingers to calculate.

"That's forty dollars a foot," she whispered to Grandma.

"And that's only the beginning," Mr. Glen said. "When my patron sees your fine work, your exemplary work, I'm sure he will offer you a commission every year."

It was as if he knew exactly what they wanted to hear. I kept stealing glances at Henry, but he was determined to play along.

"We should celebrate," Henry said.

"Yes, yes, a toast to our bargain." Mr. Glen scuttled off to the room where his boxes were kept and came back with a bottle of whiskey. There was a moment of quiet, and everyone turned to look at Grandpa.

He stood up with his fists clenched behind his back, weighing the duties of hospitality with moral obligation.

"Come now," Mr. Glen said in a meeker tone. "A drink to our partnership. It's only a custom."

Grandpa made the briefest of nods, and Mr. Glen poured whiskey for himself, Grandpa, and Uncle Jeremiah.

"To a long and productive partnership," he said, raising his glass and drinking. Grandpa raised his glass silently and watched Mr. Glen drink; then he threw his whiskey onto the fire in the middle of the room. A thin orange flame leapt up as high as a grown man and then sank down. It left behind a brief smell of burnt sugar.

Ida gasped with delight as if this were part of a potlatch show.

"It is our custom," Grandpa said, and then retired to his own room at the head of the house.

Uncle Jeremiah gave Mr. Glen a hard look, said "To long prosperity," and did the same.

I'd heard him say to his boys a hundred times, "Whiskey was invented for the purpose of stealing from Indians."

"Oh dear," Mr. Glen said, looking rather forlornly at the fire and then at Uncle Jeremiah walking away from him.

I gave Henry a satisfied nod. Whatever the museum man was looking to steal, he wasn't going to get it from us with whiskey.

"Come, Mr. Glen," Henry said cheerfully. "They're just being traditional. It's bachelors' night to wash up."

He scooped up an armload of dishes, and on the way past he whispered, "Charlie and I are going to distract Mr. Glen. You need to search his boxes while we do."

I nodded and went to work.

"Ida, do you want a cribbage game or a story before bed?" I matched my cheerful tone to Henry's. "Good night, everyone."

Grandma and Aunt Loula had followed their husbands to their rooms, so only the boys were left. Mr. Glen reluctantly set his bottle of whiskey on the table and joined Henry and Charlie at the dish tub.

I knew better than to rush Ida to sleep. If she guessed I was up to something, she'd stay awake for hours and pepper me with questions. I unbraided her hair and gave it the gentlest brushing. I read a chapter of *The Wizard of Oz* in my slowest, most sleepy voice. I kept skipping sentences in the book because I was trying to listen in on the conversation in the kitchen, but their voices were lost in the washing and stacking of plates.

I was nearly to the end of the chapter when Ida asked, "We're going to be all right now, aren't we? Now that Daddy and Grandpa can sell their carving."

For a moment, I didn't know what to say. I hadn't realized Ida had been worried all this time too.

"I'm going to be an artist," she said. "You'll see. When I'm bigger I'll do my fair share."

"Don't worry," I said, stroking her hair. "We've got each other." I blew out the candle and listened. The men were still in the kitchen. There was one lamp on the table, and the fire had burned low. I tiptoed softly around the edge of the common room in the middle of the house, keeping to the shadows. Mr. Glen's room was a small rectangle separated from the rest of the house with a wooden screen and a curtain for a door.

I was a dozen steps from it when the men came out of the kitchen. I froze and hugged the darkness by the wall.

"Now," Henry said briskly, "how about a card game?" He set down a deck of cards and two cups.

"Don't mind if I do," Mr. Glen said, sitting at the table. "Will you drink with me?"

"I'm not bound by tradition," Henry said. He sat across from Mr. Glen and dropped a dishcloth on the floor by his feet. Charlie, on the opposite side of the table, stared at Henry with his mouth hanging open. I couldn't believe it either.

"Charlie will deal," Henry went on smoothly. "Would five-card draw be acceptable?"

"Yes, perfectly." Mr. Glen poured a generous glass of whiskey for both of them.

"To partnership," Henry said.

"Indeed," came the reply.

Henry raised his glass. As soon as Mr. Glen tipped

his head back to drink, Henry lowered his glass and quickly poured its contents onto the dishtowel. Charlie hid a smile behind a fan of cards and opened the bidding.

As soon as all eyes were on the table, I slipped into Mr. Glen's room. I propped open one of the curtains enough to let a narrow triangle of light fall on the floor. There were four large crates and two small ones, plus a large leather suitcase and the canvas knapsack.

One of the large crates was already open. I peeked in and found the owl mask, an old painted spindle whorl, a few of Aunt Loula's baskets, and a large collection of rocks, each one labeled and wrapped in muslin. I lifted the corner of the other three crates and learned they were empty. One of the smaller crates was also open. It held rows of green bottles, twenty-three in all and a space for the missing one. Whiskey, and obviously he wasn't drinking it himself. I moved to the second smaller crate, but it was nailed shut. I took out my folding knife and slipped a blade in beside the corner nail. I wiggled the knife to loosen the nail. It came up with a squeak like a mouse in a hawk's claws. My heart hammered in my throat. Mr. Glen said, "Oh dear," and stood up.

Charlie laughed. "It's only a mouse."

There was a clink and glug of another glass of whiskey being poured.

"Try not to think about the mice," Henry said.

I heard a rather girlish giggle, and then Mr. Glen said, "To all creatures great and small."

"All creatures," Henry replied. There was more laughing and the slap of cards on the table. Then Henry said, "You'll be leaving tomorrow?"

"Yes, yes, regrettable, but I must move on. I'll see your two pennies and raise you a nickel."

"I'm out," Charlie said, setting his cards down.

"I'll see your nickel," Henry said, sliding his money into the pot. "Where will you go?"

"North," Mr. Glen said. Someone gathered in a handful of coins. "Whose deal?"

"Mine," Henry said. "Will you go to Neah Bay or across the strait to the Nootka?"

"Both."

Cards slapped on the table.

"Perhaps you would find a letter of introduction useful?" Henry asked.

"That would be very decent of you," Mr. Glen said.

"You are far from home with no kin to defend you," Henry said. "It's only right that we assist you."

"How very kind. To friendship," Mr. Glen said, and I heard the clink of one glass against the other.

"I'm sure you'd do the same for us if we were guests in your home," Charlie said. There was a less than polite pause in the conversation. Mr. Glen made another nervous giggle.

"Yes, of course, I would do the same."

"Don't worry," Henry said. "I'm sure you will find generous hosts as far as your journey takes you. It is our custom."

"Wonderful news."

"Ante up," Charlie said.

Someone shuffled the cards and coins dropped on the table. I decided not to risk opening the second box. I lifted a corner to see if it was full and heard the muffled chime of glass bottles.

What could he possibly need two cases of whiskey for? I went to the leather suitcase. It held two pairs of pants neatly rolled, the notebook Mr. Glen always wrote in, and a large sheaf of papers. I took both to the parted curtain to read them. The notebook was all descriptions of land forms and rock types, a wildcatter's notebook. I flipped back a dozen pages. He had been surveying the whole coast up from the Columbia River. I closed the book and smoothed the sheaf of paper on the floor.

The first thing to catch my eye was the Washington State seal. I traced my finger down the page, reading as fast as I could: land lease . . . mineral rights . . . 50 years . . . exempt from all liabilities and damages . . .

At the bottom of the page it said Ozette, Washington, 1923, and there were lines for signatures. So that was what the whiskey was for. The next page was identical except for the name at the bottom: Neah Bay, Washington. The following pages named Nitinat and Alert Bay, nine tribal lands in all. I reread the list twice to fix the names in my memory, and then put the papers back where I found them.

I snuck back across to the room Ida and I shared, wondering how I could let Henry know I was done. I thought a moment and then poked Ida in the ribs. Nothing. I tried again. She let out a little groan and rolled over.

"Go to sleep, silly. It was a dream," I said in what I hoped was a voice that sounded sleepy.

It worked. A minute or so later, Henry yawned loudly and said, "You'll want to start early. Best get some sleep." There were mumbles of agreement and the sound of cards and pennies being cleared away, and then the house fell silent.

## 16

## *The Letter*

The next morning, I woke up before Grandma did and found Henry at the table with pen and ink writing a letter of introduction. I hurried over and told him what I'd found the night before.

"So he means to lease the land and tap oil."

"Yes, and there was a whole paragraph about liability and damages. It said there could be explosions, landslides, noxious clouds, and watershed poisoning."

Henry nodded. "They tried to drill south of here once, maybe fifteen years ago. There was an accident and a spill. Every fish in the river died. It's been more than ten years and they are still dirt-poor down there."

"We have to do something," I said, pacing the length of the table and back.

"We did," Henry said. "Nobody signed a lease for our land. This letter will warn Grandpa's cousin Solomon Jackson, and then he'll know not to sign a lease either."

"But what about the others?" I said, still pacing. "There were eight other towns on the lease papers. We have to help all of them." I turned to face Henry. "We have to go to those places and get there first. We have to warn them."

Henry set down his pen and gave me a tired look.

"It's nearly a thousand miles to Juneau. It's the middle of October. I would need a dozen strong men to make that trip in midsummer." He looked at the ground. "I'm sorry. It's just not possible."

Grandma came in before I had a chance to answer. I fussed at the problem silently while I helped Grandma set out breakfast. There had to be a way to stop him. If there really was oil up here, Mr. Glen was not the last wildcatter we would see.

Susi would know what to do. I wished I was still with her at the post office, and then it hit me. What could be simpler?

An hour later, when Uncle Jeremiah was getting the canoe ready for the trip up to Neah Bay and Henry was helping carry the boxes, I found Mr. Glen writing a letter.

"Are you going to take all the things we sold you

along to Neah Bay, or will you send them back in the mail?"

"I'll keep them with me," Mr. Glen said. "Why do you ask?"

"When you go up north, you won't find people living in a longhouse as we do. Almost everywhere people live in the government houses, and they're very small."

I looked at Henry for support and he said, "It's true. Most tribes that have a longhouse don't live in it anymore."

"So there won't be room for all your things in the little houses," I added.

"I see," said Mr. Glen.

"I could take them to Susi's post office," I said in a voice I hoped was not too eager. "I'm going there anyway. I promised Susi I'd bring her medicine plants."

"It so happens I have a very important letter here," Mr. Glen said. "To my patron. I need to draw funds to complete my trip."

"I can have it in the mail for you this evening," I said.


An hour later, I headed south with the letter safe and dry under my coat and the crate of rock samples strapped down in the bow. I felt like a warrior with prisoners in my canoe. I paddled hard and fast, turning out plans as I went. First, I would take all his rock samples and replace them with fakes, and then I would forge a new letter saying not to send money, that the trip was unsuccessful and no oil or gas could be found.

I paddled the whole way without resting and my arms were trembling when I landed on the beach at Kalaloch, but in my mind, I was already singing victory songs. I untied the crate and used the rope as a tumpline to carry the crate on my back. I trudged up the beach, resting once on a drift log, and then the rest of the way to the post office.

Susi was closing up for the day. Her smile behind the polished post-office counter was the best feeling of coming home I could remember. In that moment, I was positive everything would work out perfectly. I let the whole story of Mr. Glen's visit gush out of me like water pours out of the mountains in spring, and her praise for my cleverness was better by far than the warmth of her fire and her good elk stew.

We were settled at the table upstairs when I got to the part about switching the rock samples so his partners would think he was not able to find oil. Susi got up and walked over to the window even though there was nothing but darkness to see. She let an uncomfortable silence follow my plan.

Finally, she turned to me and said quietly, "We must not do this. We will not."

"What?"

"That man gave you a sealed letter and package to carry. He trusted you. This letter and box is the property of the person he sends it to. You will not open them."

I couldn't believe it—Susi, talking like a school-master, like an Indian agent. "He stole from us," I shot back. "And he means to steal more. He lied to us, claimed to be an art dealer when he's nothing but a prospector."

"You will not tamper with the mail."

"Whose side are you on?" I shouted. "Just watch, he'll take the oil, poison our waters, and leave us with nothing. If you stand by and let him rob from us and kill our salmon—our salmon, Susi! Who will protect them if we don't? If you do this, you are no family of mine!"

Susi walked to where I sat and put her hand over mine on the table. Her hand was exactly the same as mine, down to the shape of each fingernail. A tear fell on the table beside our hands.

"You are my mirror," Susi said. "When a white man comes to the post office and calls me squaw or spits on the floor in front of my feet, I look at your face and know that I am beautiful." She paused, then her voice grew stronger like the grandmothers'. "I gave my word to defend the mail, defend it equally. Do not ask me to lie. Do not ask me to be one of them."

Susi stayed there with her hand over mine and waited for me to speak, to look at her, but I couldn't. She was right, and I hated it. I was right to stop Mr. Glen, and I knew it. I felt as trapped as I did in all those dreams where I heard my name called only to find a stone blocking my way.

"Raven tricked people," I said at last. "He told lies, but he saved the people."

Susi sniffed back her tears and said, "It's true. What would Raven do?" She went to her cot and slid out the drum. She began to play, not a song, just tapping and listening, as if she were asking her drum a question.

I went to my coat and got out the diary from my pocket. I opened to a fresh page and drew my father's Raven mask. I wrote down everything I remembered my father ever saying about Raven, not only the stories but what makes Raven think the way he does. I was four pages into it when I noticed Susi looking at me.

"What are you writing?" She came and sat beside me. "Can I look?"

No one had ever read my writing before. My face grew hot, and my heels drummed the floor as I watched her read.

"This is incredible," she whispered.

I stared down at my feet. "The schoolmaster always said I had good penmanship."

"It's not the letters, Pearl, it's the words. Clear. Simple. I can hear your papa's voice when I read this. Hear him as if he's in the room with us now." She turned to me. "You must do this," she said firmly. "You must do much more of this and show people."

"But—"

"The people need this as much as they need good fish and warm houses."

"But what if I'm wrong? What if I forgot some really important part?" I imagined the whole row of old women who sit in the honored position at all the feasts. I imagined them shaking their heads and clucking to each other about that pathetic Pearl Carver, a girl who didn't know her own stories properly.

Susi put an arm around me. "The truth that you know is enough. If you put your words out in front of the people, they will give you more stories to tell. You just have to—"

"Have the courage of my ideas." I let that thought echo in my head. I turned my diary back to the page with the whaler's petroglyph, the page with the storyteller's open mouth.

"Susi, do they have a post office at Neah Bay and Nitinat and Alert Bay?" I named all nine names on Mr. Glen's list.

"Yes, of course," she said.

"I know the words I have to start with." I turned to a fresh page.

*To all people who count the Pacific Shore their home and the salmon and cedars their kin:*

*A trickster is traveling among us. A small man who claims to be an art dealer. Do not be deceived by his money or his whiskey. I have learned the truth.*

MAY 1999

That was the first of a thousand letters to tribes and gov-
ernors and senators and presidents. Later, I became an
editor of an Indian newspaper, and one of the authors of
the Quinault and Makah dictionaries. I wrote a volume
on medicinal plants and made sound recordings of the
old songs. For seventy-five years, words pulled my life
like a sail pulls a boat.

"Gram," Ruby says, breaking into my thoughts. "I've
been working on something, a surprise, and I want to
show you." She thumps her backpack to the ground by
my feet and yanks open the zipper. She lifts my hand and
silently sets a warm soft square in my palm.

I trace my fingers across the surface to see what she
has given me. I don't need my sight to tell it is woven
work. Wool. The first few rows are loose and lumpy, but

each one that follows becomes smoother, more confident. In the center, I feel a raised circle of wool. I gasp in wonder.

Ruby bounces from foot to foot beside me and then blurts out, "It's Chilkat weaving, Gram, just like your mama used to do! Well, not just like, hers were bigger, obviously. But it's the real thing with goat wool, thigh-spun yarn, and the warp is wound around cedar."

I trace the circle again and again, and my heart drums with joy. It is my mother's weaving exactly: the circle, the feel of the wool, the faint smell of the natural dye.

"How did you learn this?"

"From the Internet."

"No way!"

"Way! I found this lady up in Alaska, and she found the last Chilkat weaver, and she learned from her before she died, and she makes the blankets now, and there's a book and a website and everything."

I shake my head in amazement. The one piece I had never been able to find in all my traveling and writing. All this time, there was a weaver, and I never found her. Suddenly, I miss my mother as I have not missed her in decades.

"I always wanted to learn, to teach you and your mom."

"Oh," Ruby says in a huffy voice. "So saving our

language and testifying to save our fishing rights and serving on the tribal council for twenty years just aren't enough for you? Jeez, Gram, don't we have a tradition about being humble and grateful or something?"

Respect for seniors is not what it used to be.

"I wrote a grant for my school project," Ruby went on. "Janine up at the museum helped me. I'm going to spend the summer in Alaska learning how to weave the way our ancestors did, and we'll never lose the learning again."

I smile, picturing Ruby in her saggy jeans and pierced nose concentrating on a loom for hours. Who would have thought my rebel, my drummer girl, would treasure the old ways so much?

"Thank you," I say, and hold out my arms to hug her.

She steps in for only a second to kiss my cheek, and then shrugs it all off. "Really, Gram, it's hip to be retro."

"What is this on the back of your weaving?" I ask. My fingers tell me it is plain wool cloth and a flap held shut with a button.

"Oh, yeah." Ruby goes back to her bouncing. "I got with the whaling commission, and they agreed you should be the one to bless the whale with eagle down. I know the pocket is supposed to be stitched to a full Chilkat robe, but honestly, Gram, it would take me two million years to finish a whole one. So I made this little piece into a pocket, and you can wear it around your neck."

I shake my head. "You should wear this, not me."

"But, Gram," Ruby says, her voice raising a pitch higher, "I don't know the blessing in Makah, not the whole thing by heart. You should say it. We couldn't even have this whale hunt without you. You're the girl who remembered."

I take a deep breath and search for words to persuade her.

"You're right. I will do the blessing. But you"—I reach a hand up to find her shoulder—"you should wear this weaving. You learned how to do it. You thought and worked and prayed over it. That gives you the right to wear it."

I hear a little sniff and feel her nod her head. She bows in my direction and pulls off her baseball cap. I lift the woven pouch that holds the eagle down for blessing and place it around her neck. Already she is standing taller, like a princess.

"Walk with me, Ruby Carver, daughter of whalers."

We make our way down to the beach and through the crowds that have gathered. I hear shouts and laughter and the click and whir of cameras.

"Auntie Pearl!" I hear the shout and heavy tread of

Henry's grandson, the one they call Tiny. He is so tall I feel like a kindergarten child beside him.

He throws a beefy bare arm around my shoulder. I smell sweat and seawater.

"Here's your whale, Auntie," he announces so everyone will hear. "Here is the whale you've been waiting for."

He leans down and whispers, "It went exactly the way you said it would. Our whale rose her head up to look at us, and then she rose again. And I knew. It felt exactly right."

He pauses and draws in a breath. "Like the thing I've been waiting my whole life for and didn't know it until now. Come look, Auntie Pearl," he says, taking my hand. "She's beautiful."

I walk forward through the crowd. The whale's shadow falls over my shoulders. I remember the copper-green shine of the whale on the petroglyph at the seal hunter's beach. I reach out my hands and press them to the whale's skin. I feel warmth and life press back.

# Author's Note

A cedar does not have one taproot but rather relies on a multitude of broad and shallow roots that intertwine with the roots of other cedars to remain upright, not as a single tree but as a grove, an interconnected forest. Stories grow in this way. There is no single origin for this book but a weave of threads that has brought me full circle more than once in my life.

## CONNECTIONS

As a fifth grader, I saw the Raven stories told and danced by Chief Lelooska and his family at their longhouse in Ariel, Washington. When the dancer pulled the hidden string that split the mask open to reveal the sun, it seemed as magical to me in the firelight as any movie special effect. I never dreamed I would grow up to be a teacher on a reservation where similar Raven stories were told. Yet only a dozen years later I was on my way to Taholah to interview for my first teaching job. The sight of the Quinault River flowing into the ocean captivated me as no other landscape had before. The Olympic Peninsula has some of the best-preserved stretches of wilderness beach and temperate rain forest in the United States. It is a unique and stunning ecosystem, receiving fifteen feet of rain a year and nurturing trees that can live more than a thousand years. I was equally captivated by everything I learned about the local culture from my students and neighbors. Their enthusiasm for traditional stories, music, and dancing made me curious about my own history, including Irish ancestors who, like the Quinaults, fished for salmon and struggled to keep their own language and culture alive.

During our daily read-aloud time, my fifth graders once asked me, "Why is the story never about us?" launching a long conversation about why having not just generic Indian stories but a story that was about the real life of their own tribe was so important. We talked about how books are made and who makes them. In the end, Ilene Terry, who often summed things up for her classmates, said, "I guess nothing is going to change unless somebody here grows up and writes that book." I did not imagine I would be the one to grow up and write the book, but here I am, full circle again. Now Ilene is the teacher at Taholah Elementary, where most of my former fifth graders are the parents of current students.

## CULTURE AND RESPECT

Many years of research and hundreds of revisions went into the making of this book. Historical fiction can never be taken lightly, and stories involving Native Americans are particularly delicate, as the author, whether Native or not, must walk the line between illuminating the life of the characters as fully as possible and withholding cultural information not intended for the public or specific stories that are the property of an individual, family, or tribe. With help from the historians, curators, fishermen, artists, and carvers I've spoken with over the years, and in particular with the help of Kathy Kowoosh Law, a Quinault and Makah historian, and Veronica "Mice" James, the Quinault language and culture teacher, I've attempted to walk this line with care and respect.

For example, there are secret rituals involved in whale hunting that belong solely to members of a whaling family. With a girl as my narrator, I was able to describe the whale hunt from the perspective of someone who, because of her age and gender, was an outsider to that information, leaving the preparatory rituals a mystery, as they should be. Many characters from the local mythology are referenced in the story. One of the most striking things to me about my time among the Quinault was the legacy of story characters that lived so vividly in the minds of my students. None of them ventured out in the dark, swam in the ocean, or wandered alone into the forest. They could describe in lurid detail what would befall them if they dared. I know many of these stories, but they are not mine to tell. I have alluded to the Pitch Woman and the Timber Giant and a few others, trusting the reader to conjure their own frightening scenarios and leaving the full telling of these stories to the people who have a right to share them.

I have referred to the Nuu-chah-nulth as Nootka in this book. They live on the west coast of Vancouver Island and are closely related in language and economy to the Makah. They were called the Nootka in the 1920s, and I have used the name here for authenticity. Throughout the book I have chosen names and spellings of the era as nearly as I can determine them, recognizing that often there are multiple names and spellings for a town or tribe and that some names are now considered incorrect.

# WHALING

Ozette, the site of Pearl's story, is a former village site of the Makah. It was occupied by whaling families from prehistoric times to the 1930s, when it was abandoned for its lack of proximity to a school. It is also the site of an important archaeological dig, which provided many of the artifacts housed at the Makah Cultural and Research Center in Neah Bay. A visit to the museum with my students brought me to the question that launched this story. For the Makah, whaling is not a job. For generations, it was the lifeblood of their economy and the cornerstone of their spiritual and cultural life. The Makah voluntarily gave it up in the 1920s. I was haunted by the notion of what that would mean, not on a broad scale but at the level of one family's everyday needs. Subsequent visits and conversations with staff have been key to my understanding of what whaling meant and continues to mean to the Makah. The frame of the story, with Pearl as an old woman witnessing the resumption of the whale hunt, is based on the historic day in May 1999 when the Makah successfully completed their first traditional whale hunt in seventy years. In this way, Pearl is a tribute to Native grandparents everywhere who work to keep cultural memory alive.

## POTLATCH

The potlatch is the most distinctive custom of the Indians of the Pacific Northwest. It is both a social gathering and an important business event. They were traditionally given by a high-ranking chief to mark an important occasion, such as a birth, death, or marriage. Guests of every social station, and even slaves, were invited to the potlatches, where they were served a lavish feast; entertained with games, contests of strength, songs, and dancing; and presented with multiple gifts. Before outside contact, the gifts were furs, copper, carved masks, Chilkat blankets, and slaves. At the time of my story, a mix of modern and traditional gifts were given. The host of the potlatch would speak, sometimes at great length, about what the feast was honoring. At the birth of a child, for example, a name or names would be given, an inheritance established, regalia received, and the rights to certain songs, stories, dances, and masks described in detail. The guests served as witnesses to the legal transactions announced at the potlatch. The gifts were a payment for their witness, with the expectation that they would remember and uphold the rights established at the potlatch. Both Canada and the United States suppressed potlatching from the 1880s to 1951, confiscating potlatch gifts and arresting those who participated. This forced the practice underground for a few generations, and the details of how a potlatch is given have evolved. For example, they are now commonly held in school gyms. But the custom of Native people gathering to sing and dance and distribute gifts and remember who they are remains strong from the Olympic Peninsula all the way up the coast to Alaska.

## PETROGLYPHS

In the 1920s, logging roads were built all over the Olympic Peninsula, and car ownership was fairly common. However, Ozette Beach was not and still is not connected to a road, so canoe was the primary mode of transportation. There is a small tract of reservation land at Ozette, and the surrounding coastline is part of the Olympic National Park. There are park trails along the beaches where Pearl mended her canoe and discovered her petroglyphs. They are some of the most scenic hikes in the region, but harsh weather and quickly rising tides make them dangerous for inexperienced hikers. The petroglyphs in the story are my own creation, but the Wedding Rock petroglyphs can be seen on the beach about a mile south of Ozette. Rock art of this kind is found all over the Pacific Northwest, although often not in easily accessible places. There is no agreement among Native and non-Native scholars about the purpose of this art form, so the meaning and use of the ancient stone carvings remains a mystery even for those who dwell closest to them.

## EPIDEMICS AND ECONOMIC CHANGE

One of the reasons that the meaning of the petroglyphs was lost was the catastrophic death toll among the coastal tribes from unfamiliar diseases. Smallpox came to Neah Bay in the spring of 1853. The disease ravaged the town and surrounding villages for six weeks. There was no count made of the lives lost, but I met a senior at Neah Bay who said his grandfather had told him that when a person sickened with the little red spots, there was no hope. They went right away to the beach to lie down in the sand so that when they died, their body would be carried away by the tide. He said, "There were not enough living to bury the dead."

The influenza epidemic of 1918, which took Pearl's mother and baby sister, affected not only Native Americans but the entire world, and caused between 20 million and 40 million deaths. Most of those who fell ill were otherwise healthy adults who succumbed to the disease quickly, sometimes dying within hours of the first symptoms.

Pearl's desire to keep an object belonging to her mother, and then to her father, and her belief that those objects would speak to her reflect not a cultural practice but an individual and deeply human response to sudden loss and overwhelming grief.

The 1920s and '30s were a time of great upheaval for

the entire nation, and the tribes of the Pacific Northwest were no exception. Many traditional village sites were abandoned either permanently or intermittently as people moved to find work in the timber and fishing industries. Before labor unions took hold, many of those jobs were fraught with peril for workers of all backgrounds. Sometimes Native and immigrant communities lived and worked together in relative harmony. Other times there was friction. The incident in the movie theater was from my own imagination, yet every Native reader who has read that scene has said, yes, I remember this—both the deliberate shunning and the choice to respond with humor.

## ART COLLECTORS AND
## NATURAL RESOURCE MANAGEMENT

I lived in Germany shortly after my time in Taholah, and my neighbors there were intrigued to hear I'd lived on an Indian reservation. Most had read a bit of the history of the American West, an interest sparked by collections of Native American art and artifacts in the museums of France and Germany. Their curiosity got me thinking about and researching how totem poles and canoes and ceremonial robes came to be housed half a world away from their makers. The history of artifact collecting and curio selling is a long and mostly sad one. In setting my story after the heyday of museum and exhibition collecting, I gave my characters a chance to approach a collector with the benefit of experience, which allows them to see through his ruse and protect not just their regalia but also their natural resources.

There is no Shipwreck Cove on the Olympic coast, although several ships have run aground on its shores. Natural gas, coal, and oil are present in the region but are not abundant enough to make extraction worthwhile. The history of exploitation of Native tribes for their natural resources is also a long and painful one. But one of the things I admire most about the tribes of the Pacific Northwest is their longtime championing of self-determination of natural resources. Joe DeLaCruz was the chairman of the Quinaults when I lived there and was a well-known pioneer in this cause. He was the key player in the showdown at Chow Chow Bridge—a civil-rights story that I very much hope will be written by a Quinault author. An account of the resumption of whaling also cries out for a full telling by a Makah writer. There is a wealth of tales living among the tribes of the Pacific Northwest, along with the centuries-old cedars and pristine waterways. I can't wait to hear what they have to say in a story of their own.

# Resources

## FOR YOUNG READERS

Lelooska Foundation, Ariel, Washington. lelooska.org

Makah Cultural and Research Center, Neah Bay, Washington, and its museum exhibit leaflet, "The Makah Tribal Council," 1979.

Normandin, Christine, ed. *Echoes of the Elders: The Stories and Paintings of Chief Lelooska.* New York: DK Ink, 1997.

Normandin, Christine, ed. *Spirit of the Cedar People: More Stories and Paintings of Chief Lelooska.* New York: DK Ink, 1998.

There are exhibits of art and artifacts from the tribes of the Pacific Northwest in many museums and art galleries around the world. Here are a few you might visit:

American Museum of Natural History, New York

The Burke Museum of Natural History and Culture, Seattle

The Field Museum, Chicago

National Museum of the American Indian, Washington, DC

Royal British Columbia Museum, Victoria, British Columbia

FOR OLDER READERS

Cole, Douglas. *Captured Heritage: The Scramble for Northwest Coast Artifacts.* Norman: University of Oklahoma Press, 1985.

Jensen, Doreen, and Polly Sargent. *Robes of Power: Totem Poles on Cloth.* Vancouver: University of British Columbia Press, 1987.

Kirk, Ruth. *Tradition and Change on the Northwest Coast.* Seattle: University of Washington Press, 1986.

Kirk, Ruth, with Richard D. Daugherty. *Hunters of the Whale: An Adventure in Northwest Coast Archaeology.* New York: Morrow Junior Books, 1974.

# *Glossary*

With two exceptions the non-English words in this book are in the Quinault language. Historically, the Quinaults did not have a written language; however, in the late 1800s when historians came to study the Quinaults and collect their art and cultural artifacts, they also recorded their language using a notation system developed in France by the International Phonetic Association. This system uses Roman letters plus extra characters to represent sounds not found in the Roman alphabet. For example, a question mark is used for the glottal stop—the pause in sound when you say "uh-oh."

For students in the Taholah School District, Quinault language and culture is a core subject. These students learn Quinault using simplified phonetic spellings, which

I have replicated in the first list of words below. Following that are the Quinault months of the year. These are written in the International Phonetic Alphabet, most commonly used by scholars and researchers.

**Chitwin**—Bear

**Nah-gwee-nau**—You are loved

**Oo-nu-gwee-tu**—Hello

**Hamatsa mask**—A group of elaborate and very heavy masks are used in a series of dances that tell the story of a person held by a cannibal spirit. Considerable prestige is associated with the performance of the Hamatsa dances.

**Quelans**—"Mind your *quelans*" is a common phrase meaning "mind your manners," but also "be respectful of your position in the group," "have respect for yourself," and "have pride in your culture."

The numbers from one to ten are: **pau, saali, chakla, muus, tsilax, sitacha, tsoops, tsamus, tagwil, panaaks.**

The Quinaults begin their year in April to coincide with the vernal equinox and the return of the spring salmon runs. The months of the year are:

**Pangwuh?am Huhnsha?ha**—Time When the Geese Go By (April)

**Panjulashxuhtltu**—Time When the Blueback Return (May)

**Pankwuhla**—Time of Salmonberries (June)

**Panklaswhas**—Time to Gather Blackberries (July)

**Panmuu?lak**—Time of Warmth (August)

**Ts okwanpitskitl**—Leaves Are Getting Red on the Vine Maple (September)

**Pan?silpaulos**—Time of Autumn (October)

**Panitpuhtuhkstista**—Time When Clouds Are Covering (November)

**Autxaltaanem**—After the Sun Comes Back (December)

**Panpamas**—Time of Cold (January)

**Panlaleah-kilech**—Time of the Beach Willow (February)

**Panjans**—Time of the Sprouts (March)

Chinook jargon was a trade language used by the tribes of the region and also French and Russian-speaking trappers and traders and English-speaking settlers. Like any trade language, it was grammatically simple, borrowed words from a variety of sources, and was spoken with much local variation. Missionaries and researchers made some effort to record Chinook in the Roman alphabet, but it was never widely used as a written language.

**Cheechako**—Newcomer

**Skookum**—Powerful

Chinook is no longer spoken. However, many place names in the Pacific Northwest come from this language. For example, the Skookumchuck River means the Swiftwater River.

# See-oh-kwee-al—Thank You

In my first year as a fifth-grade teacher at Taholah Elementary, my students asked me why there was never a book about them. We had a long conversation about why it was important to them. That conversation was the genesis of my life as a writer, not just of this book but all of them. My first and most heartfelt thanks goes to those children named at the beginning of the book. I learned so much more from you than I ever taught.

I was very fortunate in those first years of my teaching career to be mentored by some of the most amazing women I have ever met. They not only showed me how to be a community leader and professional woman in the world, but also modeled the kind of spouse and mother and grandmother I hoped to become. Thank you, Pearl

Capoeman-Baller, Crystal Sampson, Kathy Kowoosh Law, and Veronica "Mice" James. Kathy and Mice were kind enough to help me find reliable cultural research, make suggestions about key details in the narrative, and verify the Quinault language words.

I am grateful to the entire community in Taholah, who welcomed me so warmly. As a relative newcomer to the continent and a descendant of orphans, it was a revelation to spend time among people who have lived on the same ground for thousands of years, in walking distance of all their relatives, with family stories reaching back generations. You made me curious about my own heritage, which has made my own family's life immeasurably richer in music and stories and dancing.

The resumption of whaling was a key inspiration for this story, and I am grateful to the Makah Nation for having kept their whaling history alive for all the generations it took for the whales to recover from near extinction by industrial whaling. Thank you to everyone who worked so hard to restore whaling rights to the Makah and to all who labor in the vineyard of self-determination of natural resources for Native people. Your gain in control of fishery, forestry, agricultural, and mineral rights is an opportunity for us all to learn alternatives to managing the world around us.

My most vivid childhood memory of a school field

trip was the one my class took to Ariel, Washington, to hear the stories of Chief Lelooska—a renowned carver and artist, the adopted son of Chief James Aul Sewide of the Kwakiutl. We were welcomed into a firelit cedar longhouse, blessed with eagle down, and entertained with numerous stories. Each tale was accompanied by drumming and dancers in elaborately carved and animated masks and button blankets. It was living history at its finest, and it made a deep impression on me. I am grateful that Chief Lelooska kept his promise to his elders not to take the stories to the grave with him but to share them with coming generations. I am even more grateful to find that nearly twenty years after his death, Lelooska's brother Chief Tsungani and the Lelooska Foundation are carrying on this valuable work for a new generation of schoolchildren.

I am indebted to my parents, who are unable to this day to drive past a museum of any kind and not stop for a visit. They nurtured a habit of inquiry that has served me well. I am grateful to the many people who preserved and recorded the culture of the Pacific Northwest tribes for future generations. Thank you to my editor, Jim Thomas, for listening so generously, and to the entire team at Random House, who have been so supportive in giving voice to communities that are easy to overlook.

Thank you to Andrea Burke, who shared her thoughts

on author notes, and to her colleagues, the school librarians of the Beaverton school district, who provided me with a childhood full of books. They continue to provide my own children with all the books they need, and wonderful library programming as well. We are particularly grateful for the Newbery Clubs, the Oregon Reader's Choice Awards, and the Oregon Battle of the Books.

Most of all, thank you to my husband, Bill, and our four children, who make room in our lives for stories.

## *About the Author*

ROSANNE PARRY spent her first years as a teacher in Taholah, Washington, on the Quinault Indian reservation. There she learned to love the taste of alder-smoked Blueback salmon, the cold mists of the rain forest, the sounds of the ocean, and the rhythm of a life that revolved around not the clock and the calendar but the cycle of the salmon running up the river and returning to the ocean. While there she never met a child who could not tell her a story—usually one with a monster of epic proportions. The writer she became has everything to do with the people she came to cherish and the land between the Pacific and the Olympics, where stories seemed to grow out of the earth all around her, tall and sturdy as cedars.

To learn more, please visit RosanneParry.com.